LOVE
Is the Drug

LOVE
Is the Drug

• A NOVEL •

SARAHBETH PURCELL

ATRIA BOOKS

New York   London   Toronto   Sydney

ATRIA BOOKS

1230 Avenue of the Americas
New York, NY 10020

ISBN:0-7434-7615-8

First Atria Books hardcover edition February 2004

10 9 8 7 6 5 4 3 2 1

ATRIA BOOKS is a trademark of Simon & Schuster, Inc.

Designed by Helene Berinsky

Manufactured in the United States of America

For information regarding special discounts for bulk purchases,
please contact Simon & Schuster Special Sales at 1-800-456-6798
or business@simonandschuster.com

For Dad

Acknowledgments

Gratitude to . . .

Mark K. for listening, for exchanging ideas assisted by red wine and late-night studio talks about everything from music to writing to art for those years when it looked like I might always be an expert on starving artistry, for insisting I was a writer ("damnit!"). You are my mentor in many ways and I am forever in your debt. ("Two fists in the air! Yesss!")

My agent, Clare Alexander (and Kate Shaw and all at Gillon Aitken Associates), who were my first angels of mercy. Thank you for working so hard to make this happen, for being so kind and supportive.

Publisher Judith Curr for giving *LITD* a chance, and my editor Emily Bestler (and Sarah Branham, John Paul Jones, Anne Harris, and all at Atria/Simon and Schuster) for nurturing me, for believing in me, and being open to my stream-of-consciousness ideas shared in four-in-the-morning e-mails. You can join me in my "research" for future novels anytime. Emily, you are a rock star.

My father, always my biggest fan, for playing music at three in the morning on school nights and allowing me to stay up and talk about the dichotomies and fine nuances of art and life at age five and beyond, forever influencing my unending thirst for music, knowledge, passion, and intelligent conversation.

My mother, for her strength under the most difficult situations, for the fiery red-headed spirit she passed on along with her artistic breath, and finally for, when I was a child, relating the story of her courtship with my father, which served as a fine inspiration for a very specific portion of this book.

Abby, the best big sister ever, for dropping the phone and homemade cards ("Just like Joan Wilder!").

Weston for being a gargamel and crouton and a fart.

Mon and Ivy for so very graciously feeding me a last supper of sorts. (Next time it's on me.)

Mary Alice Harbison, who deserves credit beyond what I can give. I thank you for sticking your neck out for me and making time when you didn't have much to spare.

Dear and departed Toby, for teaching me more about real love and devotion than anyone ever did before or has since.

LOVE
Is the Drug

Prologue

I am somewhere in between Arizona's state line and my destination. I am hardly conscious of where I am, much less where I am going. I am lying on the side of an abandoned road in the gravel next to the car, with my arm slashed from a broken Pabst beer bottle, and I'm waiting to die. I am hoping I pass out before the buzzards come to claim me. I am holding Petey in my arms. I need to bleed. I need to let this poison out.

You know how people, I don't know, talk show guests, I guess, say that you see your life flash before you when you die? I believe it happens to some people maybe, but all I am seeing are moments from benign eighties sitcoms. That part where Gary Coleman from *Diff'rent Strokes* is getting measured at the doctor's and Mr. Drummond tells him he's only going to grow a few more inches the rest of his life. Yep. That one. Elizabeth Berkley pre-*Showgirls* days in *Saved by the Bell*, hooked on over-the-counter No-Doz dancing around her room, screaming, "I'm a maniac! I'm a maniac!" Is it kosher to laugh when you're supposed to be giving up the ghost? Because that is some seriously funny shit. Oh yeah. And Spuds McKenzie. Remember him? That ugly dog with the alcohol problem who represented some beer company? Only I would have Spuds McKenzie at my suicide. I never win.

Okay, I need to get a grip. I have no idea where I really am or why I am here, but I have so far decided that living is no longer the most convenient option and that a broken beer bottle dragged across the wrist will absolve me of this shit-infested septic hole that has become my life. What was so bad? Why am I so fucked-up? Why can't I just get up and get back in the car and drive to the nearest mental health facility and explain to them that I am having a really bad day?

It's not like I got up one morning and thought, Gee, I'm just not as challenged as I would like to be. I think I will develop some major fears and paranoia coupled with the worst run of luck imaginable, sprinkled with low self-esteem, depression . . . ooh! Ooh! And *addiction,* too! Sweet! That should give me something to do!

I think that whoever came up with the idea of karma should eat shit. That should be their karmic debt to pay for promising idiotic people that somehow, someway, someday, *they will get theirs.* I'm getting mine and everyone else's. I don't have a pen to leave a note and I have absolutely no idea what my last words should be or who would even read them. And I think I'm losing too much blood to make my suicide soliloquy what I always imagined it would be. Only I could screw up dying. Leave it to me.

Top Ten Most
Irresistibly Sexual Songs

1. "I Want to Touch You"—Catherine Wheel: Does this song even need an explanation?

2. "The Dogs of Lust"—The The: I once read that the lead singer of The The turned up the heat in the studio to like a million degrees to simulate, I dunno, being in heat or what have you, and Johnny Marr was frickin' dying in there, playing his guitar over and over but once you hear this, it's all worth it. Sex should be served hot, sweaty, and dirty. So should sexy music.

3. "Gentleman"—Afghan Whigs: This song completely represents every single guy who somehow gets away with obnoxiously walking around like he's a god, which I loathe, and also somehow manages to make me believe it. Cocky guys can be fun . . . for a night.

4. "Stuck on You"—Failure: The video for this song was like a James Bond movie but with gymnasts instead of Pussy a Lot or whatever the fuck her name was. When I saw Failure play this live, my very first desire was to find a trampoline close by and show off my impressive tumbling abilities. Flexibility is sexy. Both literal flexibility and figurative, as well, now that I think about it.

5. "Physical"—Nine Inch Nails: When Adam Ant, whom I adored as a very young stereophile, played this song, it was kind of creepy, S&M humorous-type music. It just made me laugh like his song "Strip" did. It seemed like a cartoon for sex. But when Nine Inch Nails covered this

3

song, I was about nineteen when I heard it, and I wanted to jump out of my skin. If this version had been first, I would have been much younger when I "left Virginia" as the cherry-poppin' saying goes.

6. "Machine Gun"—Slowdive: I want, just once, to be in an intimate moment and have no concerns about what I look like, what he thinks of me, what I'm doing there, what I will say in the morning, what he'll tell his friends, what I'll tell myself if he never calls me again, what he'll pretend to want from me, what he'll think about my inability to control my noise level when I am in the act of enjoyable sexual activities, how I might romanticize the moment for the rest of my life, how I might regret the act once it is done, how he might think my body moves out of tempo, how I might not like his tempo, how there might be absolutely no good reason why I should be there with him at all except that this song happens to be on and it makes me lose all defenses. I want, one day, to turn some music on, turn the lights down low, and truly lose control with someone. This one song almost makes me feel like maybe someday I could.

7. "Stars 'N Stripes"—Grant Lee Buffalo: I think the lyrics of this song somehow mix a nice sexual encounter with a protest against swastikas and hate crimes or something, but it doesn't matter. The voice, the rhythm, the video-camera innuendo make it perfect. Perversion is completely subjective anyway. That must be the favorite phrase of perverts like me.

8. "Summertime Rolls"—Jane's Addiction: Yeah, the Ecstasy reference is obvious, but I just like the idea of actually being sober with someone and having such a nice sensation that I feel like I'm on drugs. I bet this is really about oral sex. It has to be.

9. "So Real"—Jeff Buckley: I don't have to explain what ninety percent of female Jeff Buckley fans probably did alone in their rooms to this song. It's a given.

10. "Good Morning"—the Dandy Warhols: I want someone to growl sweet things to me like this. He could be saying anything as long as it comes out like a snarl. Every girl dreams about a bad boy with a good side. I dream about a bad boy with a good side . . . who can maybe play guitar.

PART I

. . .

The Game of
Life and How to Play It

• 1 •

The Rules

I'm in a Rite Aid in the Valley and Peter Cetera is playing. I am singing along while I'm in line buying exactly three postcards, a bottle of Evian, a lighter, some butter, and a metal-barreled round hairbrush. And I know the fucking words to "The Glory of Love." Every single one of them. Okay, so *Karate Kid II* was overrated. But Peter Cetera was a genius in a bad Eighties bomber jacket, singing the theme song. I saw Cetera once at a carnival. His wife looks like you would think Peter Cetera's wife would look. Like a bleached-blonde California silicone-enhanced ditz twenty years his junior. But, bless you, Peter, for "The Glory of Love." It's just the kind of bad radio song I need to relate to right now. Not quite as respectable as Billy Joel, not quite as horrific as Michael Bolton.

There's this pudgy black-haired little girl at the Good Humor Ice Cream stand inside the pharmacy who is yelling at the acne-covered Latino ice cream man because she wanted the other kind of fudge ripple in her three-scoop cone. She has the air of a forty-five-year-old CEO in New York City who has been jilted by a cabby. She is maybe seven years old. This California girl is jaded beyond repair. My turn comes up in line.

"A pack of Marlboro Lights and a pack of Marlboro Ultralights, please."

I gave myself away right there. No one says please in the Valley. Or thank you. Unless it's in a sarcastic tone when the coffee is two minutes late and they want the head of the server. You got me. I'm not from here. But I need the Ultralights. I need something to separate myself from him, pretend that I'm not on the same path of self-destruction. Pretend that I care just one percent more about my blackened lungs to buy the "lightest" version of lung cancer available. David wants the Lights, to show that he isn't totally hard-core anything. Wishy-washy. Fucking Libras do it to me every time.

"How old are you?"

"Twenty-four."

"Can I see some ID?"

I get carded to this day, and I am now twenty-four, five days ago. I feel like I'm seventy half the time, so being mistaken for someone less than eighteen has gotten old by now. Once I show the counter girl my ID, and the two old bitches behind me have sighed their L.A. sigh that everyone has learned in the Valley, she lets me go. I sort of shimmy out of the pharmacy, feeling very proud of accomplishing something. He'll be so happy. David will see that I care enough to help him smoke himself to death.

I'm walking and trying to light a cigarette at the same time and traffic here is like a game of fucking Frogger. Dodge the cars, watch for bullets. I am getting a buzz from one puff of my Ultralight cigarette and I have to put it out. All my bright ideas make me sick. As I head over past the 7-Eleven, I'm thinking of what else is on my internal list of things to do to be a good person today, and I'm overwhelmed. But I got his cigarettes. I got the butter. Now I can bake for him. He will love my cookies. If he loves my cookies, he will love me. If he loves me, I am worthy.

I open the gate to the little white duplex on the little dead end street, and tiptoe to his door. I can hear the TV blaring. I can hear the stereo's sound effects from the video game he's been engrossed in for the last few months. He won't even notice I was gone. So now I must tiptoe inside. He can't notice when I'm there, he has to notice when I'm gone. These are the rules I have made up for David to need me. If I'm noisy, he will want me to leave. If I break something, he's better off without me. If he says the house is too small, it means that I am too big. I take up too much space. I need to figure out how to shrink myself. I need to become like rice paper, like origami, so he can fold me up and put me in his pocket until he's ready to unfold me again.

When I shut the door behind me, David glances up from his game.

"Hiya, sweetie."

"Hi, baby."

"How was your run?"

"Uh, okay."

I dodge cords and clothes on the floor and hand him his pack of cigarettes. He still hasn't really looked up from his game.

"Thanks, hon."

"Sure."

I shuffle papers, open and close drawers, try to seem like I have something to do while he's busy saving his universe there on the computer. I look over at the bottle of Cuervo on top of the fridge. I can't start drinking yet. It's only five. He'll think I'm an alcoholic. And I am so not an alcoholic. I never drink at home. I only drink when I'm on vacation, or when I'm bored or when I'm depressed. My dad is the alcoholic. I'm just . . . young. But God, I need a drink. I need to relax. I need to stop feeling like David doesn't want me here, like he doesn't like me, like he's just humoring me. I have to stop asking stupid questions like, "What's your favorite color?" and "What's your mother's sign?" I have to stop being young. I have to get jaded. I have to be cynical. I have to stop speaking. I have to be invisible. He likes things that don't really exist.

"What's wrong?"

He knows I'm a basket case, but I am this way because of so many things. I have a right to be uneven right now. It's my father's sickness, it's David's disinterest, it's that I'm twenty-four and I still haven't really figured out if I want to live or not. It's my tendency to choose the wrong times to talk. It's that with David, it's never a good time to talk. It's that I love this bastard so much I am becoming everyone I ever hated just to be nearer to him. It's that he doesn't want me near him anymore. It's that I just want this one thing to be okay. It's that it never will. It's your fault, David. I am a mess because you won't let me clean us up. You would rather remain on the floor, spilled, tracked over, something that would have made a nice conversation piece, a thing of beauty, if someone had allowed it to. You would rather be broken glass in my feet than the looking glass I peer into every day. It's that you don't care what's wrong, David. I try to hold back the tears as I look up from the twice-cleaned countertop.

"It's my dad."

David doesn't look up from his game.

"What about him?"

"He's not getting better."

Silence. No, I take that back. Not silence. There is a happy techno sound coming out of the stereo, because he is winning his video game. David's character is fairly powerful by now, and he has all these spells he casts on his opponents and each spell has a specific sound to it. And this sound means that he gained something. A weapon, money, a slave, whatever. Life is good. David is happy. He looks up triumphantly. Uncomfortably.

"That sucks."

I try to fold into smaller pieces when he looks at me, so the space around me looks bigger. So he doesn't think I take up much room at all. I suddenly want to be like the treadmill you can fold up and put under the bed.

"Yeah. He's basically . . . dying."

David gives me a blank look and turns back to kill some more creatures. I tiptoe to the bathroom and shut the door. Turn on the bath. And start to sob. How can I ever compete with an immortal character? Why do I want to? Why is it necessary for me to find the one person in the world who wants to die alone and try to force him to change his mind? This is my brand of attention. I need this attention most.

Top Ten Reasons
I Cannot Leave David

1. He needs me.

2. I think I need him.

3. I am in love with him.

4. I have to make him love me again.

5. He is too fucked up to find someone to be with him now, and I won't let him die alone.

6. I am too jaded for dating around anymore and I hate dates and I hate guys paying for dinners and expecting pussy in return and I might as well settle down now.

7. We have great sex. Did I say great? It's fucking amazing.

8. We have really good sex. It counts for two. It's that good.

9. We are both very shy and very bruised from love and we both don't trust people so we might as well be distrustful and miserable together.

10. We have a lot in common. Like cooking. And music. And books. And sex.

· 2 ·

Life After God

I'm on the phone with my friend Karen. I'm trying to get to the bottom of my relationship with David, again. She is already sick of my obsessing, again. She is telling me to move on, again. She is telling me to dump him, again. I am giving her another blow by blow of an exchange we've had, again. She's annoyed, again.

"Tyler, you had a life before David, didn't you? Get it back!"

"What did we used to talk about, Karen?"

"What do you mean?"

"On the phone. What did we discuss before David?"

"God, this is so sad. I can't remember."

"Karen, I just can't figure out what I did before I met him. I can distinctly remember buying a book of *One Hundred Card Games for One.*"

"Tyler, that should say enough right there. That purchase speaks volumes. You can't go on with life and forget this guy until you actually *get* a life."

"Well . . . it's not like I don't have things going on. Dad is struck with this thing, this horrible disease that he got because he had a fuckload of fun in his twenties and thirties . . . and hell, in his forties. His liver is eating itself. His liver is being eaten away. And all I can think about is: What do I do if David never speaks to me again? What will I do with my life?"

"Tyler, get a grip. Who the hell does he think he is? He's a loser. He has no job. The guy doesn't give a shit about you. And I'm not saying that to be mean. I'm just saying . . ."

"But you don't understand, Karen. He's so talented. Fucking unbelievable. He toured with everyone who was anyone in the early nineties."

"Tyler! Key words here, hon: 'anyone who *was* anyone.' So he opened for some bands forever ago. Whatever happened to the Screaming Trees? And Soul Asylum? And where are the Smashing Pumpkins now? And does anyone *care* where they are? I think I saw that D'Arcy chick from the Pumpkins vee-jaying on MTV last night. Or was she the one who got arrested for accepting heroin delivered to her doorstep via FedEx?"

"No, that was one of the chicks from the Breeders, I think. And don't knock the Pumpkins. Or the Breeders. Show some respect."

"What are we talking about?"

"Karen, he's just depressed. He thinks all the good times have been had already."

"Well, shit, you've had the worst life I know of, but you don't treat him like dirt."

"He doesn't treat me like dirt. Do I really have the worst life you know of?"

"Yes. Congratulations. So when was the last time David actually asked you a question?"

"Like what?"

"Like 'how are you?'"

"Uh . . . I don't know."

"Has he ever asked how you are?"

"Yes, he used to."

"Before you went there to be with him. Before you were a real thing there in his house. Before he had to actually deal with you even when he didn't want to."

"Karen, this isn't helping."

"No, Tyler, this is true. He was awesome to you before you schlepped out there to live out your big fantasy. Because you were a fantasy. You were long-distance lovers. So David created you in his head to be exactly what he wanted you to be. He designed your profile just like he does on that computer game of his. He decided what your smile was like. He decided how much you liked to talk, how often, at what pitch. He decided when he wanted to fuck your brains out, and you didn't ask for more or less because he was fucking his hand along to his image of you. He could turn you off whenever he wanted. With the flick of a switch. And then when you went to be with him, you asked for something he couldn't give you. A little bit of his life. A little piece of his space. He loved the idea of being with his fantasy of you. And you came and ruined the whole thing by being human."

"Karen, you can make it seem as small as you want. But I know that he loved me. For a little while."

LOVE IS THE DRUG

"Okay, fine. Whatever. Maybe he loved you. But obviously he knows that he can't deal with that now."

"Well, neither can I. I can't deal with the fact that he would rather curl up and die alone than be with me. I can't deal with the fact that he doesn't think to open car doors for me, that he pulls all my covers off in the middle of the night, that he gets annoyed when I want to talk about stuff."

"You can't deal with being treated like a dog."

"No, I just want him to want me. And don't you dare start singing Cheap Trick."

"Tyler, how did you end up with this guy again?"

"He was just sort of . . . an accident. A friend of a friend introduced us one time when I was in L.A. We just instantly knew we were right for each other."

"Ty, do you know how fucked up all of this is?"

"It wasn't fucked up then. It was like an old-fashioned mail order bride kinda thing. . . . Letters and phone calls and presents and yearning from a long distance . . . it was romantic. Well, sort, of. And anyway, I *am* fucked up, remember?"

"Oh, yeah. I keep forgetting. So anyway, we were talking about me now."

"We were?"

"No, Tyler, that's my point. We're always talking about this lately."

"Karen?"

"Yeah, what?"

"Do you think my dad will see me get married?"

"Oh, God, Tyler. I dunno."

"Maybe I just want to cling to David because I want my dad to see me get married."

"Sweetie, there is no way in hell David is ever going to marry anybody. He is incapable. You are trying to find any excuse to understand why you are in love with a passive-aggressive unavailable guy. It's not because your dad is sick. It's because you are."

"Thanks, Karen."

"Anytime. Tyler?"

"Yeah?"

"What do you really want?"

"I want someone to ask me how I am and really mean it. I want someone to really care what the answer is."

"That's not much to ask."

"Yeah, I know. Oh, hey, Karen, I think I know what I want to do with my life."

"Go ahead."

"Airline hostess."

"Let me guess . . . to be able to take off to California and see David again, right?"

"No! Well, I guess, yeah."

"See? You're sick. You need help."

"I miss David."

"I miss you before David."

"Good night."

"Hey, Ty?"

"Yeah?"

"How are you? Are you okay?"

"Karen, if you were only a man, things would be so perfect."

Top Ten Reasons
I Let Guys Treat Me Like Shit

1. Low self-esteem. This is the excuse everyone uses, though.

2. Dad treated Mom like shit. Once again, not very original, that one.

3. They treat me like a princess at first, showering me with compliments and promises and then about two days after they see that they have me hook, line, and sinker, they start with their asshole act and I've already fallen in love with the prince they once were.

4. I expect guys to treat me like shit. It's become this dance I do where I'm constantly whispering under my breath, "Okay, when will this one fuck me over?" And when you have a bad attitude, bad things happen.

5. I have never finished a whole Deepak Chopra book, and I have this superstition that if I did, all of a sudden, everything would go like some Persian Rumi love story. The problem is that I still can't manage to get through a whole book without going, "Bite me, Deepak."

6. I've always seen guys who are really nice to girls all the time as either pathetic, or liars who are guilty of a multitude of sins and are just being nice to cover up. I have dated losers, guys who have no jobs, who have no communication abilities whatsoever, who have told me straight-faced they would never care about me, guys who ignore basic hygiene or common courtesies, who cannot keep their dicks in their pants, who won't ever

remove their dicks from their pants, and more. But I refuse to date a pathetic guy who lives for my every desire.

7. I am codependent. That is my first language, and even when I'm in a foreign country such as a nice guy who has no major addictions, when I get comfortable, I begin speaking my native tongue and I turn him into a passive-aggressive slob or an addict of some sort.

8. You know what? Strike that last one from the record. Fuck them. I don't turn them into anything. They're that way already. That still doesn't mean I'm any good at choosing playmates.

9. I like Aimee Mann's music too much to have a normal, happy life.

10. At least they realize that I exist. If I don't let guys treat me like shit, I won't be involved with the ones I like on any level because they are not capable of being friends with me, and they are not capable of treating girls well unless the girl treats them like shit, and I can't do that. When I meet one of these types, like David, I know immediately. They're like this offer of oxygen in a room where everyone has learned to breathe recycled, dirty, boring artificial air. And I know they are bad for me before I ever speak to them, but I also know that I need them. Even if only for one uninterrupted hour. I need their brand of attention.

· 3 ·

Does Your Daughter Pet?

David is watching me come out of the bathroom, dressed all in white. I am subconsciously trying to be his virginal protector, I'm sure. But it feels like I'm trying too hard. I am wearing eyelet. I am wearing ballet slippers. Or what appear to be ballet slippers. They make me feel shorter than I am. David is tall, and I like the feeling of him being taller, of having to reach up to put my arms around him. I like his wider girth. But I don't like feeling short, even though I do want to be smaller, to stay out of his way. I want to be long and thin and wispy, like a reed or a willow branch. I want to sway in the wind and fit in the corner. I want David to notice that I've soaked in a bath of lavender and jasmine oil, so that his hands will glide over me.

I lie on the bed and stare at the ceiling. I want to forget about Dad. I want to forget that David really doesn't want me here anymore. I want to forget that this is another one of my failures. It's all my fault and I just want to forget.

"Drink some tequila," was David's suggestion on how to cheer up. But I know that if I took a shot right now he would look at me like I was a lush. God, I probably am a lush. It's five o'clock again and I want to be drunk. Blissfully drunk. Dead drunk. I don't care, just drunk. I never understood before what Dad saw in drinking. All those years, I thought he must be crazy, absorbing the liquid until he stumbled around, in a half daze, saying half-important things. Drinking always just made me sick before. And then I learned how to do it. Sort of like learning how to live in a relationship that will never work. You pretend you don't need it, you pretend you can go on without it, you pretend that it is just what's good right now, and that right now is all that matters. The olive in the bottom of your glass. The one compliment, "You look pretty." Gin and tonics won't say "I love you" and neither will he. But they will help you keep busy. Worrying. Do I drink too much? Do I care too much? Am I going crazy? Am I giving away that I really am this drunk, this in love?

David stands from the couch and looks at me all funny. I can't ever decipher what his looks mean. I think I just said I needed a hug. He opts for kissing me. He touches me in the way that David only touches me when he wants to be nearer. He starts to pull off his shoes. If David's not wearing his comfy black slippery shoes, he's wearing thick socks and these insulated booty things he ties on his feet. David is always cold. Bad circulation. His hands are always clammy. His forehead never feels the right temperature. And everything lately makes him feel colder. I always blame myself when he starts feeling sick again. I always think it's something I've done wrong. Some-times he outright blames me. At least once a day he gets to feel-ing funny. And he has to lie down. And after a few minutes he comes up with the culprit, which usually has something to do with me being there. It's the wine we drank at my request, it's the coffee he made for me that he had a sip of, it's my perfume that I'm not even wearing. I still wonder if when I'm not there he ever blames his video games for his illness. Is it ever Lord Blah Blah Blah's fault his neck hurts?

But he's not feeling sick right now. And I have to take advantage of this moment. We don't speak when we are preparing for sex. We undress silently. Separately. He won't help me with my zipper. He's got his own zippers to worry about. I am trying to figure out what prompted this action. I am always initiating something physical, only to be turned away most of the time. Does he only want it when it's his idea? And then I wonder why I initiate it so often. Am I really one of those girls who thinks that sex equals love? But there's no time for that. All that matters is that David wants it. David wants sex and so I am needed for something.

I start to unbutton my white eyelet dress. I pull my hair tie out. I try to unhook my bra, but David has undressed and is already against my chest. He pulls the bra off quickly, and slides my panties over my legs. He is grinning his Cheshire cat grin. He feels like a naughty boy. I think inside David still thinks all sexual acts are bad. All sexual thoughts are dirty. And that's why he's so open about them. He feels like a rebel. He likes breaking the rules set for him by that fucked-up lady who raised him, who perverted him, who controlled him. Every time he says "fuck" he's giving his stepmother the middle finger. And with me, sex is just escape. My family didn't talk about it, but it wasn't completely off-limits. Just off-limits around them. Mom and Dad don't kiss, they don't touch, they don't like each other enough to do things that bring each other pleasure. So anything sexual to me is another step farther away from the Tracer family and our rules. And I am running as fast as I can in the other direction. I want to kiss all the time. I want to hold David's hand until it crumbles away. I never want to let go.

David stares at my crotch with relish. He knows that I spend hours preening for him. That I shave every last hair because it's a fetish of his, and an OCD habit of mine. I hate hair. I despise body hair. And not having any body hair makes me less real to David, makes me more like the fantasy character he conjures up when he gets this close. If only he'd look at my face like he looks at my pussy.

"I know what you need."

And with that, David is lapping at me, his tongue running over my clit and inside of me and back up again, his stubble rubbing against my inner lips. I moan that old familiar aching moan. Sometimes I wish it was all as good as it probably sounds to the lawn maintenance men outside trimming the shrubs. David is concentrating like he does when he is answering a Trivial Pursuit question. His eyes are closed, and he is playing the game. He needs to solve this problem and move on to another one. He puts his finger against my ass, and into it, knowing fully that it's the most uncomfortable, the most degrading, and therefore one of the most delightful things he performs. David, if nothing else, knows what I need in moments like this. He sits up and wants to watch me rub my fingers against myself. He wants to see me get off. I never dissected this particular desire before, but now that I see how he reacts, I think I understand part of David's fascination. He wants to watch sex happen. But he doesn't want to get too involved. It's too much of a commitment. It's easier to watch a girl get off than it is to commit to getting her off. If you start to lick, you can't just stop and say you're tired. No, not in David's world. That would be like losing a video game to fatigue. Not that I'm complaining, mind you. His dedication to my pleasure is quite a turn-on. But I can't get off on my own. My biggest weakness is this one fact. So I try and try and try, like I do when I'm alone. And I have to appeal to David for help. And this makes me feel weak, and this makes David feel responsible, and he helps, when he would really rather just watch. And when I reach a point of no return, he turns me around, my face into the pillow, and spreads my legs. He sits on my legs. He knows to do this because I mentioned it once, in passing.

When we wrote back and forth to each other, before I came out here, when we had this weird, long-distance affair, I wrote him a smutty e-mail. At his request. He was at home, sick, alone, with no cure in sight, and I wanted to be his muse. I wanted to be his nursemaid and his matinee movie and all the things you give your time to when you can't do anything else.

And the story I sent mentioned this act. Sitting on the back of my legs. The passage mentioned a lot of things, a lot of physical acts that I used to think were just ideas I had read about and vomited out on to the paper to get someone off. Sexual acts that I never really wanted involving unhealthy people acting out their fucked-up childhoods with sadomasochism, oral and anal fixations, and bizarre fetishes. But David follows that smutty passage religiously. David knew it was what I wanted more than I did. I thought I was writing it all for him, to get him off, to get him to notice me, to entice him into wanting me. But just as I always said I didn't believe in tanning beds until I actually got a nice brown color from one and felt like Coco Chanel, I always said the things that I wrote weren't necessarily autobiographical. But often they are. And David knows they are. And now I realize that I'm the actual fucked-up character playing out my screwed-up childhood and forcing him to play along, trying to master all the bad things someone else did to me. But so is David. He's the other character. The hunter.

David forces himself into me, and I yelp like some porn star gone sour, and I so don't want to sound like a cliché, but he really does makes me feel like I have to yelp out like that. The act is always the same. His stabbing always stretches me to a limit where moaning is no longer an option. He likes me to talk. He likes me to tell him what I want. And I am masochistic enough to do just that. I know what I want to say. I want you to hurt me. I want you to fuck me. I want you to tell me to shut up, to be mean. I want you to put your hands over my mouth, to violate me, to abuse me. David, I want you to kill me. I want you to end whatever this is that I have become, that makes me think that you fucking me means someone really loves me, and I want you to replace me with your immortal heroes in your games. I want to be the king of your galaxy. I want to be your Guinevere. But all that comes out is, "I want you to fuck me in the ass."

One of David's old girlfriends had an obsession with anal sex. She was molested or raped or whatever and apparently she preferred him fucking her in the ass, maybe because that big bad man in her past had made her vagina a wall of shame. Or maybe she looked at sex like David did. Bad. Naughty. So she wanted to be as naughty as possible. Break all the rules. Because we are taught, from a young age, that our bodies are not our own. Especially our genitals.

David's cock belonged to his stepmother, who would have frozen it and held it under lock and key if she could have. It belonged to his ever wandering father, who taught him to never trust that a woman could ever love him enough to make him responsible for his actions, could never cherish him enough to make him stay. My vagina belongs to Mom, who won't let me have it back from when she showed me how to use tampons and how to keep it from people out of anger, and to the first boy who actually got in, one early Saturday morning when I was too drunk on tequila and too weak to push him off of me. My clitoris belongs to my father, who I embarrassingly showed it to when I was six after I thought I might have accidentally cut the damn thing off, and to the first boy to touch it, while it was still numb, still inside the bud, while he rubbed and rubbed and called for it to come out.

But we are taught that even as we might not own those things, no one owns our other part. Our bowels are saved for bathroom jokes in second grade, and for immature jokes about gay guys in high school. We are taught not to touch, smell, taste, or even recognize what comes from our ass. Just flush it and forget it. It is dirty. If society developed a way to make the experience of shitting a thing of the past, we would forget our own humanity. Defecating is something we all have to do, our moment of dispose, our true common bond. And I think maybe that's why this girl I aspired to be like, David's ex, wanted him to invade that space. So she could own it. So she could rebel and say, "I'll decide who comes in here. That man might have taken over my other parts, but this is mine."

And David likes it because it's a no-no. It's something he can hardly talk about. It's one of the only things I am too embarrassed to discuss with him, outside our fiery pillow talk. And he likes to embrace things I can't discuss. That way I can't question him about them. I think David also likes it because he has control, and it's an animalistic control. He is the hunter, and I am the prey, being pushed into the pillow, pushed into submission. He's making me do something bad. He is taking control of his cock, and doing what he wants to do with it. He is laughing at his stepmother's funeral.

I tried it at first because I knew he liked it. It was his fetish. And I wanted to do everything he liked. I wanted to be someone he liked. But once I tried it, I gave in to the charm. It wasn't dirty to me. It hurt in a hollow, aching, ripping way. I needed something to hurt that much. Nothing hurt the same way. And so David made me a follower, too. I request acts for his sense of fantasy, for my need for abuse.

As David comes, as he sighs heavily and kisses the back of my neck, I feel better. He's actually made me forget. He pulls out after a minute and goes into the bathroom to wash off. He only washes off like that when we "go Greek," as the expression goes. With regular everyday sex, he never comes inside me, and he always just gets up and wipes himself off with a paper towel, and hands me a paper towel to wipe my stomach off. David probably never comes inside any girl, for one specific reason. Don't even get him on the subject of children. I don't think he sees any use for them at all. Children or dogs. Or explanations.

Just as I hear David at the sink soaping up, washing off the contents of whatever was inside me, inside the place I never meant for him to go the first time, as I can feel the twinge of pain that always happens when he gets rough with me at my request, and the wetness starting to drip down along with my own secretions, it comes right back. All the upset. I told David about my dad's condition partly because I was upset, but also because I needed him to notice me. I might have used my father's disease for sex. Freud would say so. So would David, but that's because he never gives me the benefit of the doubt. I got what I wanted with pity. I just got a pity fuck. I got my attention this time. What will I do for attention next time?

Top Ten
Most Sexual Things about Men

1. Their cocks. I'm sorry, but anyone who loves sex as much as I do, who sees it as an experience that goes beyond grunting and expending energy, has to realize the importance of the phallic symbol of power. I don't love all men's love muscles, only the ones I love, only the guys I like fucking. Any other man's dick is just this useless, ugly, pink wet noodle they keep trying to rub against me. Guys I have no interest in remind me of perfume counter ladies, shoving this shit you could never stomach in your face, thinking you'll somehow change your mind if you're forced into it. I love the cocks of the men I love because they become these beautiful, soft, strong stamens to my flower. When David first undressed in front of me, quickly, as I begged him to hurry and just take me, I remember seeing his little patch of dark blond hair, and then his pale, hard cock in the waning sunlight from the curtain, barely open. And it was like seeing *Starry Night* for the first time. I got to have that inside me. I felt lucky. I see David in the kitchen cutting up tomatoes, his hips moving as he chops, and I think about his big wang thang hiding underneath those black sweats, without the protection of boxers or those god-awful grippers some guys wear. I think about it moving along with his chopping, like my breasts sort of bounce when I mop off the counter, and I think I'll go mad if I don't run over there and yank his sweats down and just stare at, glorify in, taste, and touch his cock. But then I know that he'll

push me away and tell me he's busy, that he's sick, that he's full, that he's tired, and I don't do it. But I think about doing it most of the time. I know I sound like a letter to *Penthouse*.

2. Their tongues. And ditto for that. An unwanted suitor's tongue, even just shown to me briefly as he licks the froth from his cappuccino off his upper lip on our first, and God willing, last date is like seeing those films of the scientists spraying anthrax over beautiful rolling hills with gentle little lambs grazing who end up dying horrible wretched deaths because I wish I could erase both of those images from my memory. But if you like the guy, you gotta love that tongue. A talented tongue is like a talented musician. They will always have pussy chasing them, no matter how old they get, as long as they use their gifts.

3. Fingers. Never underestimate the draw of a guy with good hands. And this isn't completely based on sex, either. It's just nice to hold a guy's hand who has strong palms or long fingers or whose hand just fits with yours. A guy who bites his nails to the quick is going to be obsessive-compulsively nitpicking your faults eventually. A guy whose fingernails are really long, even if he is a guitar picker, just does not want to bend for anyone. Pretty soon he'll be doing other passive-aggressive things to bother you, like refusing to take a shower for a week, or throwing his dirty laundry all over the floor, or fucking your best friend. You know, little stuff that's

annoying like that. If he won't cut his nails for you, how in the hell do you really think you'll make his little commitment problem go away?

4. Smell. Okay, this might not be a thing as much as a sense, but guys who smell bad are worse than guys who can't kiss, or guys who come too soon. You just can't cover up a bad aroma. And there are actually some guys who smell even after they have been indoctrinated into the world of frequent showers and deodorant soap. Some guys just emit this odor that says "Don't fuck me" even if they're wearing two layers of cologne. Cologne is all fine and good, but basically if a guy showers, he doesn't need cologne. One of the things that drives me most insane about David is this very fact. He does not ever smell. I take that back, he smells like something, but it is an aroma I cannot describe very well, his scent, something nearly odorless but still there, never off-putting, always comfortable and cozy. David could seriously not shower for four or five days and all would be well. No body odor, no beginnings of beady oil on the nose, nothing. Every time I went to the toilet there, I was always washing and primping and pouring vanilla oil over every inch to smell and taste pleasing if I got so lucky as to be smelled or tasted. If I peed, I washed thoroughly. I became my own sterilization bidet, obsessed that David might taste something other than nothing . . . other than the occasional sesame oil I substituted for scented lotion because David could not stomach

perfume. He could spend a fucking hour in the toilet and I would walk in there five seconds later to nothing. No smell. As if he was a robot who didn't take dumps, but instead emptied microchips or something when he got too full. This was sexy, but also disconcerting. I went to great lengths to maintain an almost inhuman hygiene level with David and he could go for days without caring and the only thing I ever noticed by the fourth day was that his golden brown hair got a little darker, and stuck to his head. I had to live up to this, but I fancied the challenge. I still do.

5. Eyes. Honest eyes. Clear eyes. Healthy eyes. Closed, peaceful, sleeping eyes. I just like eyes.

6. Calves. There is something about seeing a guy's calves. And I don't mean in shorts, because I hate any guy in any kind of shorts. I like seeing a guy's calves because it usually means we are either in bed or he is up and about the house without clothing, and if I like his calves, I usually like the rest of him, too. I still remember one of my favorite moments with someone other than David. This guy, Sage, was a total snake in the grass who totally just wanted to fuck me. But, that being said, he had the most beautiful calves. Well, his ass was really the nicest ass I've ever seen on any guy to this day, too. But he was getting up to answer the phone after we screwed around on his couch, and he was naked, and I noticed how his calves tensed up when he walked, probably still strong from soccer playing in college a few

years before, and that was the first time I ever really started noticing body parts on men.

7. You know, now that I think about it, Sage's ass deserves a number all its own. It was this round, hairless peach of an ass, and it wasn't stark white like guys who wear shorts and get tanned in the sun while mowing lawns or throwing Frisbees, it was uniform with the rest of his body, and seeing Sage from behind was just lovely. And no one's ass has matched up since then. I could give a top ten list of bad asses I have seen on guys, though. Yes, butts can be lovely on boys, especially when they know how to use them. I am guilty of grabbing the butt during sex, and if it's nice, it makes maneuvering that butt all the nicer.

8. Stomachs. Now what's interesting here is that I am not into six-packs. In fact, I hate them. I think they're immodest and cheesy and equivalent with being knighted in England. Who gives a fuck? All the guys I have really been into have less than perfect stomachs and I like them because of this. Now, I'm not into the pregnant look by any means. Beer bellies are about as attractive as cold sores. I can deal with skinny guys who have no tummies, but when the muscles are actually visible, I feel like I'm dating Anatomy Man or whoever that guy was who used to dance around on PBS with a bad white-boy Jheri Curl, wearing this lame bodysuit that had all his organs painted on the outside. When David was pulling his sweater off once, and his T-shirt came up

to reveal his naked belly, only just full of spaghetti, a bit round and cherubic, at first I was sort of mortified, because he was just as self-conscious of it as I would have been and he quickly pulled his shirt down, but then I was more accepting. He was imperfect, and I still loved him. I loved him even more because of his belly, because he liked good food and had a weakness for something so simple and inherent. I'm far from perfect anyway. Sage hated his belly, but more specifically, his belly button. He thought it was his greatest weakness. Not his tendency to get hammered and not accept no for an answer, but the fact that his navel was really huge in comparison with his stomach. This guy I dated once, Rick, was so thin he made me feel like a wildebeest when I was hanging out with him. He was just bony and scrawny and wiry like Spider-Man and he wore these spandex clothes under big baggy clothes and I should have known I would never, ever sleep with him when he bent over without his shirt on and there was not a fold where normal people's stomachs paunch a little and the skin overlaps. I should have known right then with his stomach that things were not going to work out.

9. Chests. Men are obsessed with breasts, for the most part, and I hate my chest with such a fervor that guys actually completely ignore this part of my body out of hate by proxy. I don't know what's wrong with my breasts, but they never look like those chicks' tits in *Maxim* with the rounded tops popping out of a bustier.

My boobs don't have rounded tops and they don't really "pop" out of anything. It's not that I'm flat-chested, because I'm really not, but since implants took over the world it's become normal to expect girls to have these boulder-looking boobies. Not the size, the buoyancy. The *Maxim* girls' tits look like they're jammed full of something delicious and ready to explode at any minute, while mine look like they've settled in for good and refuse to be molded into whatever shape has become the new cleavage. So anyway, I hate my chest, and I love that guys' chests never go through this torment and that they are flat and easy to lie on. David used to love when I lay on his chest, staring up at the ceiling. I knew things were going wrong when he turned on his side while we watched movies so I couldn't lie on his chest.

10. Necks. I like Adam's apples and smelling necks and feeling clean-shaven necks and when a guy's neck is long but not gawky. I also have a penchant for vampire flicks, so this could explain it.

· 4 ·

Contact

I often make lists. Let me rephrase that. I am a slave to lists. I list the top ten everything. Top Ten Bands That Are No Longer Together Whose Members Are All Still Living. Number six is the Pixies. Number three is the Psychedelic Furs. Top Ten Reasons I Will No Longer Date Guys Who Live with Their Parents. Top Ten Lines in The Breakfast Club. I use them as a reflection pool. Top Ten Things I Want to Do in Life . . . number two: To Have True Love Reciprocated . . . I thought that was marked off. For a little while. Does it count if it lasts less than twelve waking hours?

David has said "I love you." I guess I'm ahead of some in that. But by the next day, his actions withdrew the statement. He had already changed his mind. And I had only been staying with him for two days. I flew in on a Wednesday morning. We had talked for hours on the phone the night before. It was good. He was comfortable on the phone for the first time I could remember. David was better on paper, when he would get the trust bug all of a sudden and decide to spill his guts. Usually only after I sent him a photo of myself again. He could never get enough photos of me. Not dirty, just innocent pictures. Fully clothed. Just my face. Close up. Looking into my eyes. Why wouldn't a girl want to do that for a man? It was flattering. I imagined him looking at my photo when he woke up. When he went to bed. Like I wanted him to do for me in person. Look at me with a reserved awe. Cherish me.

On the phone this last night before I met him, we talked about seeing each other in a few hours. We talked about not being able to sleep. We talked about his house still being a mess. We talked about me not caring that his house was a mess. We talked about all the things we were going to do when I got there. We talked about how this had sort of been a whirlwind romance of only a few months. We talked about silly, mundane, unimportant things. And we agreed on everything. It was uncanny. We finished each other's sentences already. We were the Just Add Water relationship come to life. We acted like a couple in love for years. He played along. It wasn't just my hyper reality. He believed in it, too. Hell, he forged the boundaries, and created new stakes to make it all more interesting. He's the one who sent for me, who insisted I make this fantasy world a reality. He couldn't wait any longer. We were already losing precious time. We had to get together and get this love business over with once and for all.

Part of me romantically wanted the plane to crash on the way to see him. At least then I wouldn't disappoint him, or myself. I would die a beautifully tragic death, and he would lament our love, my memory, how perfect I was. He would write a song about me and play it to crowds of other tragic characters. No one who's ever met me carries an impression of perfection with them. But David would. My mom cried when she dropped me off at the airport. She thought I would never return. She knew I was looking for a reason to leave home for good. David was older. And he had his own place, and a past that I could try to help him forget. We could come and go as we pleased, we could make love all night and be as noisy as we wanted. Maybe he could take care of me. I told my mother as we got coffee that I hoped the plane would crash. She sobbed and made it her moment, as I knew she would. Sometimes I think I hurt my mother for effect, too.

When I stepped off the plane into Burbank Airport, I had been practicing heavy breathing half the plane ride. I was worried my palms would be sweaty, my makeup would run down my face, that I was wearing too much makeup, that my breath wouldn't be fresh, that he would think my velvet coat was just too much, that my breasts weren't perky enough, that my butt was too big, that my last-ditch dieting efforts had been unfruitful, that he wouldn't show up at all, that our chemistry would be totally off, that he was suddenly balding and trying to hide it, that I wouldn't like him anymore merely because he liked me, that something somehow would fuck this up. Nothing in my life worked out this seamlessly. If you could call our courtship seamless. It was more the monster I created. With seams all over the place. Stitches and borrowed body parts, my new hairdo, my new, more svelte figure, leather boots I was morally opposed to, a thong riding up my butt making me feel all at once sexy and like a sellout. I always made fun of girls who did these things for attention. There's that word again.

David wasn't there, at the gate. I saw a guy who was probably ten years younger than him, who scared me at first, because it could have been him. And the way he carried himself was fiendish. Just something horrible. I had reassured David, when he doubted his looks, when he questioned my interest in him, that I was all about the way a guy carried himself. And I am. I always have been. Looks seem to be about what people think when they see your face. And your face changes with your expressions, and with age. If you're constipated, you're not going to be pretty. I don't care who you are. Faces aren't what hold you at night. Faces don't pick you up and carry you off to bed. Guys think of a hot girl as one with a great body. But a pretty girl has a pretty face. And to me, it's about general comfort with someone. The way our bodies fit together. And he was cute to me. But more importantly, he seemed comfortable. Familiar. Mysterious, but humble. He wrote me letters anyone would melt over. And then I saw him walking quickly in as I trudged down the hall to baggage claim.

David brushed my cheek and swooped me up all at once before I could say much. I think he said something like "Hi, cutie" and then buried my face in his shoulder. We had run through this plan earlier. We were both terrified, and we knew if we just hugged, we wouldn't have to say anything. We could just be there, in the moment. I held onto him tighter, and wrapped my leg around him. We stopped the flow of traffic down the hallway. We bumped into the wall. We made a scene. We were a black-and-white postcard. We were love at first sight. We were in love.

Top Ten Romantic Moments in My Life That Make All My Past Misery Worthwhile

1. David and me, greeting each other at Burbank Airport.*

*I can't remember any others.

· 5 ·

Ignore the Obvious

"The nature of beauty is transient," David repeats ad nauseum. It is his finest proof, or so he thinks, that good things aren't supposed to last. Whenever I bring up questions about his behavior, about the messages behind his body language, about the reason he acts like nothing's wrong when it's clear he's having a frickin' anxiety attack about something, he starts to quote people, or talk about artists who were never really great or who were great but who had miserable lives, or tells stories about meaningless pop culture people who died before I was born. This is one of the only places I truly find fault in our eleven-year age difference. And I think—no, I'm sure—that he does it on purpose. To make me feel young. To make me feel inferior. To show me why this, he and I, will never work.

We are in a Thai restaurant, eating Thai food, vegetarian Thai food, to be specific, and it does help matters that David and I are both vegetarians, I suppose. One less thing for him to add to the list of reasons why I am absurdly unprepared for life in general. David will, on occasion, eat fish. He says anything that would eat him, he will eat. I didn't ask about bears or lions or tigers, but I think he really just means fish in general, although I somehow doubt a tuna has any interest in David as a meal. I have mentioned that the idea of the little fishies flailing this way and that, suffocating to death, bothers me too much to enjoy them, not to mention the fact that ever since I could eat solid food I've hated anything that tastes fishy (which, in essence, means anything that swims). I might convert if David insisted. I'm that impressionable at this point.

David is downing Tanqueray and tonics like they're going out of style and he frowns when I order a second Long Island iced tea. I think he wants me to have a drinking problem. It would make it easier for him to hate me, then. To stay away from me. As it stands, I really am a good thing for him, I think, and he hates that. He hates that I try to get him to go hiking with me. He hates that I try to prod him into the laundromat. He hates that I buy him all the latest vitamins, and back scratchers and toiletries by the dozens. He hates that I want to take care of him. He hates that taking care of him is all it takes to make me happy. He hates that I drink because he won't talk, and he won't listen, and there's nothing better to do in front of these fellow diners from the Valley and the Asian kitchen staff who know David by name than to drink and forget about the fact that he hates me.

I feel like I'm at a family reunion of his long lost friends from when he had a social existence, and they're all watching us, thinking, How nice, he's got a girlfriend. They must be on a date. Aren't they cute? They all know David here. Everyone he comes in contact with on a daily basis knows him in some way. David is only truly kind to acquaintances. So they love him. And he loves having distant people love him. There's no commitment in waving and asking how your grocery baggers are doing. There's no danger in the deli guy remembering what you get on your veggie sandwich every day. You can remain the nice guy who comes in twice a week for the next sixty years and no one will ever ask more than that of you. David treats me like I'm the clerk at the local pharmacy: He knows I know a lot more about his body and ailments and habits than he would like, but he tries to keep it superficial and polite so he can pay for his itch cream and be on his way.

David cannot live his life this way. This is his monotone reply to any of my requests to speak about us. I still cannot figure out if he means that he cannot live his life always questioning things that if they were more stable or honest wouldn't need to be questioned, or if he means that he cannot live his life with me wanting to merely be a speck on the globe that David calls his existence. Okay, maybe I want to be a little bit bigger than a speck. I want to be a little bigger than Luxembourg, a little smaller than Australia. I want to be like France, but polite. I want David to point to me when someone says, "What is your favorite place to visit?" As it stands, David did a quick drive through me, on the way to some other more exotic, more foreboding country with less temperamental surroundings and no bumps in the roads. And he refuses to renew his fucking passport.

It's after dinner and we're home and David and I are drunk. I know this because I have hardly eaten all day and the Thai food was my first real meal and after two Long Island teas and one and a half scotches on the rocks, I am propping my arm against the kitchen counter to stay erect. David wouldn't admit it, but he's drunk, too. I know this because whenever he has had a bit too much to drink he acts like I am a new friend at his house and this is show and tell. He brings things out of hiding, out of cupboards and cabinets and shows them to me, to gauge my reaction. He has a picture out right now of a famous musician friend, whom he is telling a story about. The story is funny to me because I like to think of David when he was this big social guy on the road playing with crazy friends. It's also funny because he's trying to impress me. He doesn't realize that growing up around musicians made it fairly hard to impress me with this sort of thing. I just like to hear him talk.

I suppose I expect a lot of him. I expect him to love me because I am so much younger and he should feel lucky to have someone who looks up to him like I do, someone who wants to fuck him as often as I want to just talk to him about silly things. I expect him to ask me questions and give me compliments and burst into the bathroom while I am taking a bath and jump in fully clothed. I expect him to act like he's an eighteen-year-old full of hormones, but also like the thirty-five-year-old he is when it comes to settling down and being responsible. I expect him to be what he wants to be for me, or wanted to be for me when he imagined what we would be like when we were finally really together. I just know what he still imagines he is capable of, and it is so wonderful.

It is in this moment, drunk, debating about art and misery in the kitchen, that I fall madly in love with David. It is a sick, full, bursting sunshine yellow feeling that makes my feet feel heavier and my fingers spread out.

Every night for the few months we talked or e-mailed or somehow communicated before I arrived, I thought I could just be in love with the whole idea of romance. But this one week I've been with him so far has proven otherwise. He sent for me. He wanted me to bring everything with me, to move in with him immediately. I obliged fully. I brought classifieds with me to find a job here. We had it all planned out . . . sort of. And then as he started to change over this first week I'd been there with him, when he started to let me in on his secrets slowly, to let his beast come out, when he decided to give in instead of fighting the fear of this goodness, only then did I get caught up in all of it. Only then did I manage to fall in love. I'm always too late.

As I stare at his dirty brown hair, his hazel eyes, his pillowy soft lips that I watch tremble when he is sleeping, his baggy black pants and button-down dress shirt, the first new shirt he's worn in days, as I look at David with my own beer goggles, thinking he is the handsomest man in all the land, sitting on the kitchen counter across from me, lecturing me about why I am lucky and why I don't appreciate things I have, I see the reason I will never love anyone like I must love him. David is an angel. He is an angry, hurt, confused, lonely angel who plays the piano like a seasoned composer and laughs like Rumplestiltskin. He is the most talented songwriter I've met. He is an angel who sighs when I am going down on him, who closes his eyes and shakes like a little boy in a rainstorm right before he comes. He is an angel because he calls me nicknames that I know he has called other girls, but makes them sound brand new for me. He cannot help the way he loves and resents love, the way he avoids me because I am here, the way he seems guilty when he looks over from his video game at me, patiently waiting for my turn with him, the way he raises his voice over mine when I try to interrupt. He cannot help that he would rather win a game than win me. I am too easy. He thinks I am the beginner level and David is on the level right before you save the princess. David is an angel who cannot love a mere mortal like me. And I think that if he ever did love me like I have convinced myself I love him at this moment, his wings would be taken away. And I love David too much to ever ask that of him.

Top Ten Reasons
Why I Cannot Be with David

1. He doesn't hold me when we sleep anymore.

2. He doesn't love me anymore.

3. He thinks he is old and sick and depressed and done with life.

4. He refuses to communicate and I am the mouth of the South.

5. He hates that I talk and I think you should never die wishing you had said something.

6. He doesn't want children. I don't know if I want children, but I like to have options in all arenas.

7. He is addicted to fucking video games. I can't even play Pac-Man.

8. He doesn't like to drive fast, and he won't let me drive because I like to drive fast. This is a major point of contention.

9. He lives across the country and doesn't want me to be here with him anymore and does not wish to move to the South, where I live.

10. He doesn't want me with him. Ouch.

· 6 ·

California All the Way

"Which one? Enchiladas or pesto? Or my spaghetti with veggie meat sauce?"

"Any of them. Really."

"No, you have to choose one. Which one?"

"Um, whichever one you want."

David looks at me with an expression of mock annoyance. Or is it? I never can seem to give him what he really wants, no matter what it is.

"Really, sweetie, I just don't have an opinion about it. I have an opinion about everything else except what to eat," I say, trying to convince myself.

"Okay, if we have enchiladas, I can make fresh guacamole, but then we can't really have the wine. But the enchiladas will be great." David looks torn. He looks absolutely dizzied by the choices. I mean, it's clear to me in a conversation as simple as what to make for dinner that David is happier with the least amount of choices possible. He says he never regrets, but the truth is, he never wants the option. He would rather have it cut and dried. This is where you're going to school. This is the car you're driving. This is the place you will live. These are your friends. This is your overaffectionate, insecure girlfriend who wants so much to make you happy, she will tell you to make all three dishes if she thinks it will help. Because if he has a choice in the matter, there is room for error, and worse yet, room for regret. And there's a chance he might blame me, even if he doesn't say it outright. Like I said. Wishy-washy Libras. And I didn't used to believe in that astrology stuff, either. Now I find it's so eerily correct, I'm doing David's fucking charts in my spare time.

David is in the kitchen. Clanging pots. He stands up and rubs his upper lip. He sort of pinches it with his thumb and forefinger. He does this while he watches television, too. And clicks his fingernails. All whilst deep in thought. David is always thinking. And eighty percent of the time he never gives me any idea what it's about. About forty percent of the time he denies he's thinking at all. But I can always see the motor turning behind his eyes. He is still struggling with the decision, Italian or Tex-Mex? Which will it be?

David puts himself through this every night I'm with him. I love that he loves to cook, because he becomes very purposeful and proud of himself when he's got a mission that involves pleasing me. Going at the pasta, going down on me, what's the difference in the end? They're the two things that he involves me in, gives me a little choice in. So I encourage them heavily. While he wakes up, thinking aloud, What will we have for breakfast? What will we make for dinner? my thoughts to myself as I wake up are, When can I sneak in sex before he gets too tired or sick? Either way I'm always initiating the oral fixation on one hand, and he's doing it on the other. Food becomes this unnatural focus of our daily lives. We get maddeningly depressed if we run out of eggs. And sex becomes a mission for me. I think of every angle, of how I could just slip it into the mix right after he finishes the last magic spell on that monkey in his game, how I can slink over to the couch and lean down, start slowly kissing his stomach, pulling his sweats down . . . I feel like a seventeen-year-old boy who always has an ulterior motive, is always out for the glittering lay at the end of the rainbow. And I always feel so rejected when he turns me away. I get embarrassed, and then angry, and then I feel ashamed that I want sex in the first place. So I close up for the next two days and pretend that sex doesn't matter to me, when actually I'm thinking about fucking David's brains out every time I turn around. So either way we seem like two people who so want to avoid discussing "us" that we've become hermits with eating and sex disorders.

David has decided, I think, on the spaghetti with veggie meat sauce. The kitchen smells like garlic and onion and wine, but I'm not allowed any closer than smelling distance to peek at what's boiling underneath the pots. David has a very serious policy about the kitchen. Off limits when he is in it. I thought it was a joke at first, but learned my lesson quickly when I put one foot on the linoleum the first night I was there, and saw

David turn around and give me a look so ominous, I thought we were through before we had even begun. The house is small, a studio duplex. So the kitchen part serves as a sanctuary of sorts for David, away from me and my questions.

When David gets sick and lies in bed and flips through the channels, I always end up in the bathroom. That's my sanctuary. Most of the time I just turn on the faucet and try to pee. I've always had to do that when I'm nervous, which is basically always. I was a bed wetter when I was younger, so I taught myself, more like forced myself, to learn how to empty my bladder often. When I want to stay away longer, or rather, when I can tell that David wants me to stay away, I fill the bath and try to time myself to see how long I can soak before I get fidgety and have to drain the tub. It's usually only about ten minutes before I give in. I always thought I could be one of those loungy types who takes bubble baths for an hour daily while reading a trashy novel, but there's something that is not quite right in David's tub. I always get the feeling that I should drown in there. The water gets too cold too fast, his walls get too yellowed around me, the plastic shower curtain is too shiny, the lint from the towels floats on top of the bathwater and I want to sink my head underneath and romantically stop trying to float to the surface. Maybe then I'll have a fucking impact on David.

At first, I automatically assumed my "thing" was coming back, like it always does. I call it my thing because it's so unpredictable, and so unexplainable. It's the thing that made me so insecure as a child. The thing that makes me afraid to ever trust anyone completely. The thing that robbed me of so much time, so much energy, so many youthful moments I could have enjoyed instead of locking myself up in a room for months on end. The thing that made me lay in bed for days and days and days on end. The thing that years before forced me to sleep seventeen hours a day and hope to never wake up. The thing that once made me experiment with doses of pills to see how close I could get to killing it without necessarily killing myself in the process. The thing that convinced me that maybe it had become me, that the me I once knew had been swallowed whole and replaced by this half-dead person. The damn thing that keeps me from ever enjoying myself completely. The thing that landed me in a hospital eventually—not a mental hospital, mind you, a pediatric hospital at age fifteen because I was dehydrated and ghostly pale and Mom wanted to believe it was anything but what it really was. All in my head.

I nearly did try to drown in David's tub one time, actually, in one of my needier moments, when I had just found out about my father getting worse and David was showing no signs of life for hours on that computer and I had smoked about fifteen cigarettes and done the crossword twice. I was drunk on misery and being ignored and I wanted to die in a bathtub á la Jim Morrison, without the heroin, in L.A. We can't all have Paris, you know. But then I remembered the door was locked and David would never break down the door to save me, so I would probably end up in the water for a few days, in which case I would become a bloated whale of my former self before anyone discovered me and I am too vain to have his last memory of me be like that. He is a very aurally obsessed person and I would hate to disappoint him in my last act. If I am going to commit a romantic suicide in the name of heartbreak and art and love and all that, I want to die pretty. It's the least I can ask for, really.

Music used to be David's escape. He's this amazing musician, who has at one time or another been all over the world in his band playing for thousands of people. When we first met, I knew he was gifted. He can touch anyone's music and turn it to gold. But once the vocalist in his band died and the rest of the band broke up, he had to go it alone. It was too daunting. He started taking behind-the-scenes stuff. Studio jobs. Playing second-rate music. All the junk musicians take when they've given up doing what they really want to do. And I think he never really recovered his self-esteem. He has catalogues of music that could all be top forty hits, but he can't get it together enough to do something with it. He doesn't have the hunger anymore. And it makes me want to scream. That's what we shared in the first place. The passion for our art. His for music, and mine for writing. I emote on paper and I hunger for people to read it. I want to affect people. I will write stories I dream up until the day I die and live in between the spaces of sentences and paragraphs. David has decided instead to survive day to day and just play music when everything else goes silent. When there are no noises to distract him. I am afraid he will wait until he dies to really play again.

So now David's sanctuary is the game. That fucking game on the computer. That RPG, role-playing game thing that is sort of like Dungeons & Dragons and Tomb Raider rolled into one. It keeps him from the greatness he could realize and might have the responsibility to take on. His thoughts to himself when he arises have got to be, How soon can I get on that computer game without Tyler giving me an eat-shit-and-die look? He tries to explain the whole passion, that it's a way to escape, like drinking is for some people. But I know in my heart of hearts that drinking is about as good an escape as an innocent game of suicide skiing, so I know also that David's complete obsession with video games of this type, or any type, are far from healthy. And so does he. It's a crutch to save him from speaking, a way to stay away from the real world outside, the beautiful California sunshine out there that he swears is the only reason he even bothers with L.A. anymore. I mean, why doesn't he move somewhere cheaper with less crazy people and no earthquakes? At least he wouldn't risk game interruption then.

David actually says, quite convincingly, that he likes these games for the social interaction. He says this straight-faced, while he plays with and against other cyberjunkies who are online all over the world playing the same game, who maybe say two personal words in four hours like, "Let's go kill some stuff!" or "This lag sucks." He doesn't speak to anyone in the outside world for weeks, maybe months, and he still feels somehow like he has filled his social quota by just being online at the same time as a couple of thousand other lonely, game-obsessed junkies. I wonder what the statistics are on video gamers and their family history of addiction. I'm willing to bet the margin is huge. Video games are mental abuse, pure and simple. I still can't quite grasp what he sees in the whole thing, but I find myself trying to be much more interesting, much more dynamic than what's on the screen. I find myself actually dressing up in order to move David's eyes from the computer for a few moments. I am competing with Lord Blah Blah Blah. And losing. And I think I wanted Tex-Mex after all.

Top Ten Reasons I Am
Better Than a Video Game

1. I have tits. Me: 1, Lord Blah Blah Blah: zip.

2. Lord Blah Blah Blah does exactly what David programs him to do, and never asks, "What does this all mean to you?" Shit. One-all.

3. I clean David's house. And do a fucking amazing job, I must say. Ha!

4. Lord Blah Blah Blah costs ten bucks a month to keep playing. Another for me.

5. Lord Blah Blah Blah is magic and can heal himself at will. But I can make red wine come out of a white sweater and make a meal out of two pieces of gum, a casserole dish, a piece of stale bread, and some leftover jam. I am like the MacGyver of cooking. Hmm . . . that's a tie.

6. I look better in jeans. That should be worth at least ten points.

7. Lord Blah Blah Blah is too busy being a pompous little fucker in some forest, chasing monsters and casting ridiculous spells, to think about having sex. So, as bitter as I sound, I can have sex. Hmm, not sure if that's a point for me or for him. Depends on how David's feeling that day.

8. David can't turn my volume and enthusiasm down like he can turn down the game, but he can turn me on and I'll shut up faster than the volume knob can go from ten to zero. Damn, another tie.

9. I play better music than that stupid game.

10. Fuck this. I'm real, for God's sake. I am real.

· 7 ·

Half a Person

David is laying down an eight of hearts on my run of a five, a six, and a seven of hearts. I am trying to hide my excitement at having such a brilliant hand, while David bites his lip and tells me I'm going to slaughter him with the hand he's got. We are playing gin rummy on the last night I am with him. I need to go back home. Dad is sick. David is sick of me. We've already had a bottle of Pinot Noir and some pesto pizza. My buzz is gone, and we've watched a terrible video, and we've played a twenty-minute game of Trivial Pursuit that David completely reamed me on. I felt stupider in that one game than I ever did when I went to those damn honors science classes in high school. I knew nothing. And it usually doesn't bother me, because I guess I have stupid friends and they never know the answers, either. I hover around the pink areas and answer banal entertainment questions and feel not so moronic and always end up winning by default. But David is really, really well informed on history and politics and science, and I know

---

just about enough to not feel like a typical American. He knew almost every answer to every question, and the ones he didn't know were stupid questions anyway. David has so many things he's good at that it literally sometimes makes me want to scream. He uses about six percent of his talents. He is living the words "potential if applied oneself."

We only have a few hours until we're supposed to be up and leaving for the airport, so we decided to just stay up and stick it out. Neither one of us are morning people. I am convinced that David could have been the next big thing if he was a morning person. David has the talent, the ideas, the famous friends, the musical genius to be something great. An icon. David is probably the most gifted person I've ever met. There's nothing he couldn't pick up and figure how to make beautiful sounds come out of within fifteen minutes. Even me.

David makes me feel cheated as an artist about ninety percent of the time. Cheated and, at the same time, fortunate. High Art is overrated. Really, it is. And I'm not saying that because I'm jealous. As much as it stirs me to see him creating, to hear the symphonies of sound he creates, to hear his beautiful Bryan Ferry–like voice singing the high notes, as much as he says that his existence is a happy one, that he wouldn't change anything, he is fucking miserable. Most of the time. And it is true. Most people who are given those things, who have somehow tapped into the power to hear those tones the planets make and make sense of them, and make songs from them, have these monsters in them that suck the white light out of moments and force these people to make horrible choices, to treat the people who could really love them and help them like shit, to self-destruct before they ever get a chance to truly enjoy themselves, to become stories we read and think are romantic. But I watch David scowl at another artist he sees on TV with not even one-fifth of his talent living the jet-set life, and it's not romantic. He brags about knowing some of these people and I just shrug. It's sad when your life becomes all about who you met once at a gig three years ago. Who cares?

David's existence is hand to mouth. Living by whatever means necessary. No compromises, no security, no extra anything. I mean, David's fetish for paper towels is about the only thing that might be considered frivolous at this point. Well, that and the video games at thirty to fifty bucks a pop. And I was willing to live it with him, this fucking Basquiat nightmare come to life. Because the sounds he makes, the notions that come forth when he thinks, the love he believed really could conquer his darkness and self-hatred were worth it to me. But the final catch, the one that makes it impossible right now for me to be very happy about winning gin rummy or happy about being here for the next four hours comes to the surface. Because David courts his art, he thinks he will be unfaithful to her if he courts anything else. So I am a mistress tossed aside in favor of being alone with a keyboard, a pack of cigarettes, and an idea for a song at three in the morning. Or a video game that soothes him as he works songs out in his head and escapes reality for another day.

I win rummy by five points. I feel satisfied, but not as satisfied as I would have been if I had won Trivial Pursuit. David puts the cards up and grabs the remote control. The last few hours we have from this visit that went all wrong, and watching Japanese game shows and old sitcoms is not what I had in mind. I slip off the bed, over to my suitcase, grab a bundle of black things, and sneak into the bathroom. As I turn on the faucet and do my obsessively clean and fragrant routine, I realize this is the last time I will do it for David. Maybe ever. I'm not stupid. I know he has been stressed out while I've been here these past two weeks. I know he is humoring me. I know that he has already made his choice, the one I never imposed upon him in the first place, between me and alone, me and art, me and the possibility of what's better than me, between me, all new and unsure and a little bit of responsibility and the comfort of the same existence he's always had. I know that David doesn't want to deal with me. I know that these last few hours might be the last few hours he'll ever be with me. So as I slide on my black push-up teddy and my black fishnet thigh highs, I'm thinking that I must take advantage of this thing I've chased. I must make him want me one more time. So I dress in clothing I would have never worn before. The outfit of desperation. Pathetic.

I poke my head out of the bathroom door as David is staring sort of sleepily at the television. He looks at me with annoyance when I tell him to close his eyes. He actually says "What?" in the tone of a person whose last wish on earth is to be spontaneous or, God forbid, playful. But he closes his eyes after I urge him another time. I tiptoe to the bed and climb onto David and kiss his forehead as he opens his eyes. David moans.

"I feel kinda . . . sick, sweetie." No, this can't be happening.

Not on my last night. Not the last night I might ever see David again. I don't move.

"My stomach hurts . . . I just feel weird." I climb off of David and sit next to him on the bed in my getup. I look kind of agitated by this sick thing.

"But you look really cute, sweetie." This doesn't comfort me, even though it's one of the few compliments David hands out. He never seems to want to notice if I make an effort. Too much pressure.

"Well, it's all for you," I say in a sunshiny voice.

"I know. I wish I felt decent." David isn't even as good as I've become at faking sincerity. I turn off the kitchen light and come back onto the bed and whisper in his ear.

"Well, how about I just sort of start it myself and you can watch and help me when you do feel better . . ." I thought he just needed coaxing and, as modest as I am, I am willing to try anything. I am willing to try to create an ambiance that just isn't there.

"No, don't move around. I feel really cruddy." I feel more rejected than I ever have before, when I would slide down to the waistband of his sweatpants only to be pushed away.

David gets up and shuffles in his slippers into the kitchen, where he drinks a glass of water, and then some Alka-Seltzer. He moans again. I ask him if it's indigestion. If it's an ulcer. If it's the Ebola virus. What is it, so we can fucking cure you and you can give me this last night, these last few hours? David, you took away my heart, took your offer back to keep me company in life, so the least you could do is not take this away from me. David sits on the edge of the bed, while I sit on my feet and feel helpless. I try not to move too much or shake the bed as I pad into the kitchen to boil some water for herbal tea. I stand by the stovetop, waiting at the kettle because water boils so fast at sea level, as David moans some more and puts his head in his hands. He belches a few times and then moans again. Then he runs into the bathroom as the kettle whistles and begins retching like he's been poisoned or something. He's puking up days of stuff. The sound is the loudest noise that he has ever emitted. It is horrific. And he just keeps yakking while I'm standing in the kitchen, pouring some ginger tea in a cup in a black push-up teddy and black fishnet thigh highs, waiting for him to come out. I look like a misplaced hooker. It would be funny if I let it. But I'm so upset, so disappointed that I can't do anything but act like it is all normal. Status quo. This is life with David, and I will accept all of it if he will just have me.

David finally sounds like he's finished, flushes the toilet, and comes out of the bathroom like he's been beaten by this thing. He looks at me with a flushed face and says, "See?" as if I didn't believe him before. Maybe I didn't, now that I think about it. He pulls the covers off the bed and climbs in, moaning and sort of curling up into a ball as he flips through the channels. I try not to shake the bed as I climb in on the other side and watch TV with him. He's quickly fading off to sleep, and I'm realizing that he doesn't want to get out of this bed for the next week. And something in me offers to take a cab, even though it's the last thing on earth I want to do. He sounds guilty when he mumbles, "We'll see how I feel when I wake up," as if he's getting up tomorrow instead of in two and a half hours. I turn the TV off and try to sleep next to David one last time. I try to remember the smell of the green flannel sheets, try to remember how this feels, to have someone keeping me warm in bed, even if he won't cuddle anymore. I try to remember the way the moonlight comes through David's window, how the heater makes this creaking noise when it kicks on, how the fridge always groans just when I'm about to fall asleep again. I try not to cry in bed next to David in my ridiculous outfit meant to entice him that now makes me feel idiotic. I try not to notice he is already grinding his teeth while he sleeps. I try not to notice my chronic spinal condition making a return visit as my shoulders start to itch and my neck starts to ache. I try not to notice as David turns on his side and sort of wails a little in his sleep and then sounds as if he's sobbing quietly. David is no longer grinding his teeth, he is crying in his sleep, and I realize, but still try not to notice, that I feel bad for him. I want to save him from the awful place, this world he thinks he is okay in. I want to hold him right now, to wake him up and tell him that I can make everything better if he only lets me do it. I want to wake David up and say that what is happening to us is bullshit, that he is being a coward, that he is breaking my heart in the most cruel fashion possible, with indifference, and that I want to die in this bed right now rather than leave. I realize I have been praying for a 6.0 earthquake to hit us right here in the Valley ever since I landed here, just so we will be forced together. So I can stay a little longer even though this is misery. I keep thinking if only I had a little more time, David would come around. If only the earth would come and swallow us up, everything would be fine.

I sort of startle a little when I wake up at 5:45 and I can't see anything, almost like there's a fog between me and the form next to me, so I reach out and touch it to see if David really is there, if all of this really happened. David awakens and looks annoyed as I pretend I didn't touch him. He doesn't change his expression but just mutters, "You should call the cab and tell them to come now. You need to leave within the next forty-five minutes in case of traffic."

I slide out of bed and remember all over again that I am dressed like a tart and as I sit on the couch in my black teddy thing, I self-consciously pull at the straps and call a cab company to come. They'll be there in half an hour. I have a half an hour to be with David for the last time ever. I have thirty minutes to get dressed, pack up all my shit in the bathroom, all the things I primped with for his sake, to say something that matters to David, and leave his house with the shadow of a memory that might make him want me to come back. The challenge is too daunting.

David flicks the lamp on as I throw brushes and bottles in any bag they will fit in, as I slide my jeans and my big black boots on and click around the house, gathering things up as if it's all very purposeful, as if I am concerned only with getting all of my things out of the way. David's eyes are closed. He just wants this to be over with. He just wants me to leave so he can pretend I was never here in the first place. And all I want from this next half an hour is to make an impact. I want David to give me the tiniest inkling that he gives a shit. After I think I am halfway assembled, I sit on the edge of the couch, crying silently. I am trying not to be a basket case. But this is the last time I will do any of this, and I know it.

"David, this is hard, but it's worth it."

David opens his eyes as if a fly is bugging him and, if he looks at it, it will disappear. "What's hard?"

I climb on the bed where he is. "This. Us."

He almost snorts and says, "Don't get philosophical on me or I'll puke again."

I hit him on the knee lightly.

"And don't hit me."

It's obvious David is no longer even trying at "civil." He no longer cares if he shows that he has signed me off his concerns for good. I cry harder and pretend it's about my father, when I know all along it is because someone hates me so much they are actually trying to be cruel and hurtful. The man who once said that I was the best thing that ever happened to him no longer even cares that he is making me cry. He is breaking my heart. He is making me hurt more than anyone ever has because I am for some reason willing to put up with it, and I think it's somehow my fault, that I have done something to make him hate me. I kiss his forehead and hear the cab pull up. I drag my suitcases outside in the darkness as the cabby reaches for them and throws them in the trunk. I ask for a minute and walk back into the house for the last time.

"Well, I'm out of your hair." I feel like my stomach is going to eat my throat.

"Is that the taxi?" David sounds about as concerned as people do when they say "How are you?" to the checkout lady at the grocery store.

"Yeah, that's me. I'm going to miss you."

"Yeah, see you soon, sweetie." David will never be good at being L.A.-love-ya-babe. He does not do fake sincerity well at all.

"Okay. . . . I love you . . . so much." The words I promised I wouldn't say again unless he said them first.

"I love you, too." The words that don't mean very much to David, I gather.

I walk out of David's little white duplex with the little green door and try to not start bawling until I reach the cab. I am saying good-bye to him for the last time. I am making my exit and missing him already for the last time. As I pull away I am probably having my heart broken for the last time. I can't ever do this again. No one will ever be allowed to hurt me like David has.

The taxi driver tells me his life story on the way to Burbank Airport as the sun rises on the palm trees and temperamental drivers. I reciprocate with the story of David and me. It's not like I'm ever going to see this guy again anyway. And it is clear to this L.A. cabdriver that David is screwed up, that I am screwed up, that I think I need someone so much I am accepting half a person. Less than half a person. The past idea of half what a person used to want to be. I am a fucking Oprah show, only there are no hugs and understanding nods at the end of my segment. I am one of those guests she will never get through to. I am the one who has to be hauled off to boot camp and still just doesn't get it. The cabdriver basically tells me to leave him alone, that he'll come around, that any guy who was forty and was struggling and ill would realize at some point that he would be lucky to have someone like me, and I nod and sob a little and feel like this cabby will never understand that David will regret every single action in his life except me. He will never regret hurting me because he thinks he has to. And I am mostly crying because I am the only person in the entire world besides David who understands this.

I tip the driver generously for just putting up with me more than anything, and the skycap asks me how my trip was and where my final destination is. He says I have beautiful eyes and I start to tear up at this because David used to say that, too, before. At my gate there is bedlam. Frustrated and cranky passengers are climbing off the plane, other passengers are waiting in line, asking how a plane that's half-full can have a weight restriction problem, and I am standing there with tears now fully flowing, trying to understand what's going on. The flight can't be canceled. I have forty bucks left to my name and David hates me. He'll think I'm making it up if I show up back there an hour after I left. I am secretly hoping the flight is canceled, of course. I reach the desk and ask what the hell is going on. They are offering vouchers for six hundred bucks to passengers who will volunteer to give up their seats and make other travel arrangements because of the winds there in Burbank and their effect on the plane's ability to take off. This was the sign I was waiting for. The sign that I can stay longer. The sign that means that I can pretend there was a problem with the plane, accept the voucher, stay longer with David, take care of him while he's sick, and make everything better. I could have volunteered to do all of this so easily. I fight myself for the next ten minutes to do it. I come up with every excuse why it's a good idea, why I can somehow make David want me again. I fight as I give the flight attendant my boarding pass. I fight as I find my seat and sit down, numb. I fight as I look out the tiny circular window and watch the passengers leaving the plane. I fight as they close the hatch and begin their lecture on how to buckle a seat belt. I fight myself and then realize it's too late as we take off. I watch all the little houses and mountains and pools and palm trees get smaller as we get higher, as I pull farther away from the last time anything will hurt this much. And I imagine I see David lying in his little white house on his little Ikea bed, sleeping and grinding his teeth and snoring, as if I never ran into his arms at that airport, as if he never stopped being lonely for a little while because of me, as if I never made him smile or laugh or feel loved, as if I never existed at all. And I still have to keep myself from going back, even if it takes jumping out to do it.

Top Ten Reasons
to Not Have a Nervous Breakdown
When I Get Home

1. Umm...

   I can't even pretend I have any intention of being a functional human being when I return. I give up.

Part II

. . .

Being Happy

And Other Empty Pursuits

· 8 ·

Objects Are Closer
Than They Appear

It's my disease!"

I stared straight ahead at the passenger seat in front of me as Dad screamed this from the front. I repeated the word mockingly, under my breath. "Disease!" Then I mouthed it, putting my hand to my lips when I said it again, as the car pulled out of the parking garage and onto Twenty-first Avenue. When I think of disease, I think of gaping wounds, oozing sores, screaming, flailing victims, or people who suffer in a Gandhi-like way, making everyone around them feel worse because they don't show emotion. But I don't think of the reality I am seeing. Of hospital rooms that smell of disinfectant and old blood and mourning, of doctors who smile when they shake your hand and tell you things won't get better, of lists they put you on to give you someone else's guts. I thought disease was kind of like Social Security. Something I wouldn't live to experience in my lifetime.

"I just think she deserves to know, James. You're being so mean to me! All of you are!"

My mother started sobbing. She couldn't let my father have this day where he got the attention. She had to steal the fire somehow. We're all attention junkies in my family, and she can be the worst. You should see us at holiday dinners. Whoever screams loudest gets the attention. Or whoever is most animated, the most pissed off, the drunkest . . . whatever. Attention equals love in the Tracer family. Attention equals justification. Attention is more precious than gold, more important than good night kisses, more worthy than admiration. We all crave it. Some of us in more desperate ways than others.

"Mother, you're being such a fucking baby. This is not about you. This is about Dad. I know what he's saying. We shouldn't tell Judy. She's already ruined my life with gossip. Just shut up already."

Ferris scowled in the backseat next to me as we rode back home from Dad's appointment with the specialist. She gets her attention in her own ways. She likes to drink, and drink she does. Ferris becomes this Claritin-enhanced version of herself when she drinks, like a wide-eyed Kewpie doll on crack, dancing and flirting and getting drinks bought for her left and right. And she can stay up for days. I remember waking up from a drinking binge with her one time. The sun was just coming up on a July morning during our summer vacation from that all-girls school. Hundreds of people had shown up to our impromptu party when the folks went out of town one summer evening. By now they'd all gone home or passed out. But not Ferris. She had on a black motorcycle helmet and was dancing in her bra and panties along to AC/DC's "Back in Black." She was trying to wake us up to play some more. She needed more attention.

"Everybody shut up! Hello, Judy? Judy, this is your dad . . . I'm fine, honey. Everything's okay. We're just leaving the doctor's office and I wanted to let you know how I am. . . . No, I have to go to another specialist. Everything's fine. I'm fine."

Fine. The Tracer family's favorite word. And it was always a lie. Our house just burned down. We're fine. Dad's got a drinking problem. It's fine. Someone robbed us at gunpoint. Oh, we're fine. Dad's going to die. This is not fine.

Top Ten Reasons
My Father Cannot Die Yet

1. He just started to grow up.

2. I just started to grow up.

3. He doesn't look all that sick. Well, not all the time.

4. I just decided that I really do love him.

5. He hasn't met Bob Dylan and he always wanted to meet Bob Dylan.

6. I'm not mentally prepared to deal with my father dying yet.

7. I always get involved with guys whose fathers are dead or have never been around, and I have to have a dad if they don't.

8. I want my dad to live to be a grandpa, even if it's my sisters who have the kids.

9. I don't want to have to tell my children about him, instead of letting them see what they think of him for themselves. Even though I'm still not sure I'm having kids.

10. I want my daddy to walk me down the aisle.

· 9 ·

Seven Habits of Highly Defective People

It's 2:30 in the afternoon. I keep tossing and turning and going back to bed. I can't get to sleep this time. Even the over-the-counter Sominex crap isn't helping. I have to get up and do something. Dad's in the hospital again. Getting fluid sucked out of his stomach. Fluid that, no doubt, has been collecting from his liver's inability to process it. Or they'll tell us something like that. I have to get up and do something today. I've been away from David's lair only a few days and I'm falling apart. Might as well go to the hospital to see Dad. Maybe that will make me feel bad about something else. Maybe then I'll have an excuse to cry about something that's supposed to matter.

When I'm walking to the elevators, I'm sucking down the last bit of cigarette, watching some old lady whose husband no doubt is dying from lung cancer smoking underneath the Cancer Center sign. She looks like she's a slave to the thing she's smoking. Her face has those wrinkles that only come from pursing your lips around a cigarette and relishing the carbon monoxide for years. She's suffering for her past pleasure. Just like I am. David is my nicotine fix, the black spot that will soon enough eat holes where I used to have lungs. I throw the cigarette down behind me and press a button on the elevator. I have no idea where Dad is. I'll just put my finger in the air and gravitate toward the smell of karma. And the Tracer family rules.

The funniest thing about hospitals is that they're built for death. They have these beds that tilt, for those too weak to sit up without assistance. And the disposable water pitchers, disposable bedpans, disposable thermometer casings, disposable well wishes. I mean, nurses can give sympathy to thirty families in one day. Do you think all the sympathy and good wishes are sincere? I don't know. I think maybe they throw them in the basket with their used scrubs at the end of the night. Start over the next day. You know you're bad off when the nurses become really nice to you. When they remember you. Nurses don't remember people who radiate health and vitality. They think of those people as pussies with colds who want to play hooky from work. Nurses remember people who look like they need a nurse. People who are sunken in, sallow, tired, aged, frail, weak, arriving with family members in tow, who look worried and dumbstruck. That's why the nurse knew who I was looking for. She spotted me right away.

"James Tracer is in room 7729."

I might have asked what room Dad was in, but for effect I imagined that the nurse just guessed from the look on my face.

Much of my life is created for effect. I think my mother might have given birth to me merely for effect. I remember slicing my foot open on a Mason jar in the front yard, looking at the gaping, bleeding wound that was too deep and too severe to hurt just yet, and screaming for effect. Hell, it looked like it hurt. So I was expected to react accordingly. I think I might believe I'm in love with David and am allowing him to rip my heart out and stomp all over it for effect. Maybe he's just an overdramatic reaction to a situation that's not going the way I had planned. I'm chasing him, I'm defiling myself, I'm on my hands and knees scrubbing his bathroom floor and begging him to notice me for effect. It would be so easy then. Then I could take my cue to bow, let the houselights go down, and collect my roses. I pulled off a great performance of a woman with undying love for a man who loves no one. I wish I were that great an actress.

When I push the hospital door open, Dad is still having the procedure. Mom is at her post on the rocker chair, trying to needlepoint, something that requires patience, which my mother has not had since my father has been ill. Even when I was very young I could sense that my mother forced herself to have all four of us. It was her path to enlightenment. She would suffer and suffer and suffer and bleed on her cross made of cross-stitch needles and diet shakes in the name of her cause. But a martyr isn't supposed to ask for gratitude. She always forgets this point. Mom sees herself from a mirror that's twenty years old. And even then I think she has gilded the mirror a bit. She was smarter, thinner, more patient, more loving, more forgiving, more saintly in her past. And mostly all I've ever known of her is her regret. Her decision to blame her children and my dad and her childhood for her inability to make up her own mind. When she gets what she wants, she realizes how little it means. She and David are more alike than is comfortable for me to admit.

Ferris is on her cell phone, connecting with her friends, or whatever she calls it that she does when she makes plans to get shithoused again, to lose her ID at some nondescript bar, to go home with some total beast of a drunk, to delay reality for one more day. I'm not being hard on her. She hates this about herself, too. What she hates most, though, is the comedown. Reality. Waking up next to the beast. Ferris is the victim of her own good times. She is more like my father than she thinks.

My father, before he got sick, was always a wounded man. He needed my mother most in the world, and he hated her most. He still does. James Tracer is a self-made man who cannot take care of himself. I love my father like I love sad, lonely love songs. Like "Sea of Heartbreak" and "Don't Let It Bring You Down." I have two reactions to those songs, as I do with my father. I sing along and cry and think of all the good things that could be, or I laugh it off and pretend they're not playing. It's funny because it's so incomplete, this love, these songs. They could be so much fuller, but they're not. They possess that fatal potential that makes them have to fall short.

Dad had the fatal potential, too. He didn't take the time to realize that I would have but one graduation to sober up and show up for, one thirteenth birthday party that he could have

not crashed with a bottle of vodka and his pistol, one childhood he could have been present, sober, and actually awake for.
I love my father because I know that he wanted to be a top forty,
touching pop song, but he just missed the mark and became a
sad tune on the B-side. I always had the patience to listen to the
B-sides, because my cassette recorder didn't rewind. I listened, I
loved, because I had no choice. And now he's fading off, and I
can sense the pop tune coming on again. And I am so not in the
mood for it at all. I want that sad song to go on forever. I want
my daddy to stay. I want to listen to these songs over and over
and let them and him try my patience. I want to take my father
and put him on continuous play.

Top Ten Injuries I Have Endured and Lived to Talk About

1. Jumping off balcony into a bush, age two. The bush broke skin, and I still have a crack down my forehead that only I can feel. I think my mother should have known I was a suicide case waiting to happen right then.

2. Falling off bathroom vanity from standing position onto corner of wall, bloodying carpet, walls, clothes, and giving myself a nice concussion, age three. I just lost my sense of balance, my sense of wanting to be on the counter anymore. So I fell backward. I still think this is the reason I am foggy and loopy. I had to have done damage permanently. I once read that every time you even knock your head even slightly on something, your brain gets bruised. If this is true, all my past uneven actions are explainable. Totally.

3. Falling off branch into Harpeth River at Narrows of the Harpeth, age eight. I slipped off the log and was trapped underneath in the rushing water for what seemed like an hour. I remember staring up at my mom and dad and my sister and her friend, watching me drown, and quite calmly thinking, I wonder . . . I wonder if I'll live.

4. First car accident, with my dad, age nine. Dad had been drinking all night and was still sloshed when he got up a few hours later to take me to school. He pulled out of our long gravel driveway in our little green Volkswagen Bug, and flipped the thing on its side into the ditch next to the mailbox. I got a bruise on my knee, and was quite

impressed that we climbed out
like the car on *Knight Rider*. I cou
morning, and I think about that a
why Dad didn't feel very bad about
got to school, no one believed me whe
car accident.

5. Jumping on a broken mason jar, age el
which actually forced itself into my left arc
all the way through to the other side, causing
damage to the nerve endings in that foot, which
why I have no balance and am a complete klutz, ha
broken by yours truly only hours before and not p
up, and so I learned all at once two important
lessons: Karma reigns, and Never walk outside barefoo

6. Being slammed in the head with a baseball bat, age
twelve. Ferris wins again. I didn't want to pitch baseballs
to her anymore, and she doesn't like pitching. So she
was telling me in her oh-so demonstrative way that the
game was over. I passed out. I came to with Ferris
pulling my limp body alongside her and saying, "Walk it
off. Don't tell Mom and Dad, just walk it off."

7. At age thirteen, getting run over by a go-cart going full
speed, driven by my big sister Ferris. I had just arrived
home from a soccer game, so I had cleats on and shin
guards, and my sister was always trying to get me to soil
my pants, I think, so in the front yard she came at me in
the cart and managed to clip my leg. I was propelled a
few feet in the air and landed safely in a cheerleading

osition. The shin guards saved my leg and I'm still quite fond of anything with a protective plastic layer because of this.

. Second car accident, age sixteen. Returning home from seeing World Party play a concert and was a little more interested in the radio station level and my ringing ears than in the cars in line ahead of me. Slammed right into the person in front of me and ended up taking a lovely ambulance ride. My right arm is still fragile because of this, and I can never hear World Party without thinking of airbags and lawsuits.

9. Hydromyelia, age twenty. Well, actually I still have to deal with this thing, but it came on when I was about twenty and it's not so much an injury as a chronic affliction, but when I wake up at three in the morning with that itch on my neck and the pain that shoots down my spine, it feels like I must have done something wicked to my back or neck at some point in my life to feel this fucking bad. It's water on my spinal cord. It builds up in there and presses on my nerve endings, making them tell my nerves to feel all sorts of things. Itching and pain are the worst of the lot. It's fine when it's not there. It consumes my life when it is. I can't wear polyester because it makes me itch more. Then I can't wear wool. Then it's any artificial fabric. Then it's the tags on the back of my shirts. Then it's the fabric softener in the shirt. Then it's the way I'm sitting up in bed, reading, with my neck propped up. Then it's working at the computer too much. Then it's just that

I'm stressed out. Or I drank too much caffeine. There's always some new culprit that I discover, and I'll scratch until I bleed and all the skin comes off my shoulders and I've taken all the antihistamines in the house hours ago and I'm drugged out and frustrated and still itching. And still no relief. When the neurologists were doing the tests, to see what exactly was going on, I remember getting the myleogram, where they numb you with an epidural sort of shot and then shoot dye into your spine to see where the fluid collects and how, and I remember seeing this television image of my spine, and my back, and all my organs resting there while the doctor shoved this instrument through my spinal cord. My organs moved with my breathing, relaxed, trying to ignore the offending object above them in another part of my body. I remember thinking, This must be what dying is like, really. Your body has no idea it's happening because it's numb by now. When the itching comes on, I have to mind everything I do and not do anything that involves my neck or back or shoulders. Impossible. It's a bit like being elderly, really. You have to constantly take into account how your body will react to certain situations. And the pain never truly goes away. It just dulls. It's kind of like a broken heart, I suppose.

10. Every paper cut and stovetop burn I've ever had because I have experienced horrific physical pain and endured all of it, but these are the things that make me weep like a baby still.

· 10 ·

Overqualified . . . for Life in General

I just missed out on a job. I was asked to fill out another application at the staffing service because I can't choose an occupation myself so I would rather have someone who doesn't know me or what I like to force me into a position that I am likely to hate so I can blame my miserable existence on them. Anyway, I started to fill out the application for some secretarial position and something in me clicked. I turned the sheet over and just began to write.

"Hello, my name is Tyler Tracer and I am falling apart. My childhood was totally screwed up and I don't mean screwed up like normal people's childhoods are screwed up, and my dad is sick and I think he's dying, but I can't do anything about it, and it makes me mad but also angry that I am worried about stupid things like whether or not I should buy teeth whitener, instead of Dad's illness. I am twenty-four years old and I have no ability whatsoever to choose an occupation or a hair color.

Or playmates. They shit on me in the most heinous ways, especially playmates who see me naked, playmates of the male persuasion, playmates who always find some far more important game to play than real life or love or romance or even kind friend. I'm trying to quit smoking, but every time I decide to quit I decide also to stop drinking caffeine and then at about two o'clock in the afternoon I get this shaky kind of not-right feeling and I have to make a cup of coffee and then I get on the phone with Karen because I have failed to be a healthy human being for the millionth time and I need her to commiserate with me, and when I'm on the phone I like to smoke. It's kind of like when you're going by a mirror, you feel the need to look, even though you already know what you look like—it's a habit. Like smoking. On the phone. Don't ask questions, I'll do the talking here. So I am a smoker, and that might cut into my work time as I like to smoke about a billion cigarettes a day and then I quit for about a day and I am testy on that day, to say the least, so I'm going to need about every other day off. I am going through a bit of a bad patch. It's lasted about . . . twenty years. I can't remember what I was doing with my life until I was about four, so I start the timeline of misery just about there, and assume that with my lost memories of early childhood I have lost the secret to life. And one day I hope to find it. You see, I think I would be a fine candidate for your position if only I did not have to deal with other human beings. They just mess everything up completely. Which brings me to guys again. I think that maybe if I could work in an environment devoid of them, I would be okay for a while. Actually,

I take that back because I really don't like women all that much, either, as they are bitchy and bloated some days and they talk with their hands a lot and always want to know how everyone feels about them when I could honestly care less about my coworkers in general. And they try to gossip about things they really have no idea about, and lie about stupid things like whether they color their hair when their eyebrows are black and their hair is brassy blonde and every single thing they do is to please a man or to trap a man or to entice a man. And then that brings me back to men, who I cannot talk about. I cannot deal with them and work at the same time. I do not want to have an office romance, nor do I want to stumble into work sixteen minutes late in the same dress two days in a row because I got hammered the night before and had to do the walk of shame from the house of some total loser whose name I cannot remember. I do not want to dress up for a guy in the cubicle down the hall who likes to play paper football games and tell dirty jokes to the guy in the cubicle next to mine. I do not wish to deal with them at all because I am no good at playing their game. And don't tell me it's not a game that they play because it is, whether it is the game of how many of my girlfriends they can screw while I am at a party with them, or the game of how many times they can break promises to me about important shit like whether they have been married before or not, or the game of buddies being more important than girlfriends and watching a football game being so much more important than paying any attention to the fact that your girlfriend is actually leaving you because you don't pay any attention to her, or the game of not calling a girl after an amazing date because they get worried that this girl might be the one and that puts too much pressure on the situation because they have so many not-the-ones they still want to fuck, so they end up never calling the girl back even though the girl is perfect in every way for them, and the girl ends up blaming herself and never really dating normally after then. Boys like games. Video games. Football games. Mean, unfair relationship games. Drinking games. Games of all sorts. And I am tired of him being the racehorse, so I have to be the fucking thimble again and he always gets to be the banker and cheats me out of anything I earn as I go around the board trying not to land on Park Place again, because I am bankrupt from the last time he landed on Boardwalk and I offered up Mediterranean Avenue and my utilities card to the bank for him because I cared more about the fact that he would be happy that I saved his ass than the fact that I am fucking broke and I cannot help someone who refuses to pass go and collect anyway. I have no business playing games with these boys. Or working at your fine institution. I need to have a nervous breakdown right now, so please keep my application on file and I will get back to you when I figure out what I can write where it says 'recent accomplishments.' Thank you."

I wonder why I didn't get hired.

Top Ten Shitty Occupations I Have Held for More Than Thirty Seconds

1. Telemarketer. That takes the fucking cake. Three hours, twenty-six minutes. Sold nothing. Smoked sixteen cigarettes. It was cool that I could smoke while I worked.

2. Toy store slave. Kids are vicious little blood-sucking shits. They want everything and then they break it and want more. Three months, one week, half a day. Sold lots of crap no one needs.

3. Nanny. Being a parent is almost as much fun as it sounds. Seven years, two months. Sold nothing but my domestic prowess. I did learn to cook a mean plate of spaghetti.

4. Secretary. I have no hand-eye coordination. This makes it hard to answer six lines when they're ringing all at once. One day.

5. Car washer. Manual labor is not my forte. Four hours, and then I took off for an extended lunch break. I've never returned.

6. Journalist. Professional bullshitting. Anyone who says that journalism is a respectable profession is a liar and is a journalist. Six months. Then I got my soul back.

7. Waitress. Oh yes, this lasted all of an hour. Hungry people + shitty tips = no fun.

8. Census taker. I didn't even get through all the classes to learn how to ask people questions they don't want to answer. I got paid ten bucks an hour to go to the classes, though. Three days in training.

9. Makeup sales. My sister hooked me into it. You just can't paint over ugly. I didn't realize I said this aloud until it was too late. Sixteen hours.

10. Starving artist. Still holding a job in this lovely occupation. It could go on forever.

· 11 ·

Welcome to Paradise, Population: 1

"God never gives you any more than you can handle."
Dad actually says this, on the phone to a concerned
friend, about his own illness, about the disease that is currently
making his ankles swell up like baseball bats and turning his
skin the color of an alcoholic's day-old stomach bile, if it was
puked up and dried out in the sun. When he pulls his socks off
at the end of the night, he is supposed to check for swelling.
There's no genius scientific discovery going on here. If my
father's legs had drainpipes, if he could open the floodgates
once daily, yellow-greenish fluid would come pouring out.
Bucketloads. He is collecting fluid like a bulimic who has gone
straight. Like a woman with her period taking place in every
part of her body. It looks like someone beat him up and his
body is swollen with yellowish blood. James Tracer is the color
and exact moment of a bruise in the process of developing.

He is taking pills, to flush out the "water." He is taking pills to flush out the water after that water is flushed. He is taking pills so he won't have seizures. He is taking pills so that he won't get depressed about his condition. My father's liver is throwing up all its contents inside his body, and he thinks he can handle this. He thinks that God has given him a challenging *Jeopardy* question, which only he is meant to research and answer.

But doesn't the expression stop ringing true when you get something you can't handle? Obviously, Dad's body cannot handle what's happening to it. It's rebelling. Cirrhosis, the attack on his liver that's winning. I never believed old sayings like that anyway. I placed that cliché along in the same category as "We'll cross that bridge when we come to it" (the procrastinator's wet dream remark), "Pretty is as pretty does" (what kind of bullshit did the pageant mothers create with that?), and "Hard work is its own reward" (or a cool mil and a chateau in Provence, whichever one comes first).

I think my father wants it all to be true. Just like he wanted to be a Jehovah's Witness, even though even he knew it was psycho to shun birthday celebrations because of some passage in the Bible about John the Baptist. Dad wanted to be a good, upstanding Christian, but his impulses didn't quite steer him in that direction. And Mom was always the temptress, turning Dad into the staunch, unbendable preacher at home. She tried to be the strict one, but she didn't have enough patience to follow through. And Dad just felt guilty about not being around, so he pretty much gave a ruling once a month. Like a Supreme Court justice, he was kept out of the situation until it was absolutely necessary. Dad was only called in to parent when something big and expensive was broken and it would be missed, when Mom had decided to punish us with disclosure to him, or when he found out about something through one of my little sister's loose-lipped stories of the day. None of us listened to either of them anyway. I mean, how you can you look at your father straight-faced and obey him when he's teetering this way and that, trying to focus so he can look you in the eye? How can you listen to your mother when she visibly doesn't care what the outcome is as much as she cares about how our father will react to it? So I sort of raised myself. And see? I didn't handle that one very well. And God certainly didn't stop by for an instruction lesson on being a kid in the Tracer family.

Dad is answering questions on the phone like a president who's been caught playing nookie in the Oval Office. He knows everyone knows that he's sick. He looks bad. But he keeps that monotone optimism and swears he's never felt better. It's funny how no one will ask how you are when you show up to work crying, or in the same clothes from the day before, or when you suddenly take down the picture of your longtime boyfriend and replace it with pictures of your cat. No one really wants to get involved in emotionally draining situations. But when you are visibly falling apart inside yourself, when you're a literal skeleton, you might have a disease. You might be dying, and contrary to what everyone tells you, knowing someone who's dying but who's not very close to you is kind of glamorous. You can tell other people about it at luncheons where there's nothing better to talk about than acquaintances who have illnesses.

"You know, my good friend James Tracer has liver disease, and I'll tell you, I've never seen someone be so optimistic in all my life."

You can use it as a point of reference, to seem like a caring, compassionate, understanding person.

"Oh yeah, I know what you're saying. I've seen so many of those I love get ill. As a matter of a fact, my friend James is on the list for a new liver. It's just so hard to deal with."

So I'm suspicious when Dad answers these phone calls from "friends" who care. Maybe it's also because Dad is in the music business. And the music business is sort of like a monarchy in Iran. If someone well noted in your profession is sick, that leaves a little space where you just might be able to creep in. So why not call him up, see what your chances really are, get the lowdown from the horse's mouth. It all sounds so Machiavellian. And it is.

When my aunt saw my dad a few months back at a family reunion, she had Dad dead before Christmas. I think she actually wanted to believe it because my dad is the favorite child. My grandmother makes no bones about that. James made a name for himself, James bought her a couch and let her meet her favorite country music star, James eats her chess pie. And likes it. So my dad's family, although worried no doubt, manages to make us feel like we have to lie to them about how he feels, what his condition is, how well he's coming along. But then lying to protect the family is an old habit of the Tracers. We've become quite accustomed to that by now.

Since I've been back, I try to sleep as much as I can. I take as many sleeping pills as the package will allow me without overdosing. The regular eight hours isn't enough now. Sleeping is the only thing I can do where I don't have to feel bad about something, where I don't feel like I'm just waiting for David to talk to me, or for Dad to die. I wake up tonight when I hear footsteps upstairs. It turns out that Mom is in the laundry room, washing sheets at 3:00 A.M. Dad is in the bathroom, washing up. My mother is scrubbing the sheets with some space age stain fighter, looking annoyed, but mostly worried. And also she has a tinge of that martyr look. She is still in suffer mode. She whispers to me as she scrubs.

"He had an accident again."

I tiptoe downstairs and check my e-mail for word from David. Day seven and he still won't say anything to me. I think he is so devastated that the fantasy is over that he thinks he can just pretend the reality part never happened. I go back to bed and think about all the times I had accidents in my bed when I was little, and how humiliated it made me feel. My dad isn't getting better. I'm losing two people I never quite had in the first place. And I can't handle any of this.

Top Ten Best Movies
to Watch When You Are Miserable
and Lonely and Bored

1. *Truly, Madly, Deeply.* Especially if you are mourning a breakup. I still get mad because I want the girl to just go off with the ghost forever and screw all the people who think she isn't going on with her life.

2. *Dangerous Beauty.* This movie is better than Romeo and Juliet's story, because it's true. Veronica Franco is like me, only I'm not a courtesan, and I'm not a published poet or whatever, but for some reason she is me. I just identify with the story, so I went out and bought her book of letters and poetry and tried to learn Italian for about a day. Okay, I'll admit that Rufus Sewell is a pretty big draw, too.

3. *Labyrinth.* David Bowie in full eighties glam gear. *And* a magical kingdom. Enough said.

4. *Bram Stoker's Dracula.* What a piece of shit that movie is. But oh, Gary Oldman, you are our movie savior. Gary Oldman could make a movie about Kathie Lee Gifford interesting. I think I have a serious thing for vampires. And Gary Oldman. Explain that.

5. *Amadeus.* Falling in love with miserable people, thy name is Tyler.

6. *Immortal Beloved.* Ditto.

7. *Sid and Nancy.* The first time I saw *Sid and Nancy*, I thought, How fucking cool. I don't care what anyone says. Being in love and dying are the two most tragic things a person can do.

8. *Velvet Goldmine.* Sometimes I get whiny and lie in bed and watch this and think, Why can't I be a gay man? This movie is romantic the way that flowers from a secret admirer at work are romantic. They may have nothing to do with you, because they may be for the coworker next to you, but until you read the enclosure card, they're really nice to look at.

9. *Dead Again.* It's a bad Hitchcock rip-off turned early nineties thing, but it's still kind of nice to think about . . . karma and true love follow through to the next life. So maybe I'll be happy next time . . .

10. *Say Anything.* Who wouldn't want to marry Lloyd? Every girl wants to marry Lloyd. Instead we end up with that drunk guy played by Jeremy Piven, who jumps around and passes out before the party's over.

· 12 ·

Fine

"What are the two things you're going to do today?"

"Uh, call about my car getting tuned up and . . ."

"And what?"

"I forget."

"All right, I knew you weren't listening. You need to call Fran about your health insurance."

"Dad, I don't need health insurance. I can't afford it."

"Tyler, you can't afford not to have it."

"Yes I can. I just won't get sick."

"Good plan. I didn't plan on getting sick, you know."

"Yeah, but you're . . ."

"What? I'm what?"

"Old."

"Fifty is not old."

"I know . . . I mean, I'm sorry."

"What about your boyfriend? He's thirty-five."

"That's different."

"How?"

"Those fifteen years are like the fifteen years difference between ten and twenty-five. It's okay if you're thirty-five to date an twenty-year-old. But it's not cool to date a ten-year-old when you're twenty-five."

"Tyler, you are your father's daughter."

"Thanks, Dad."

"That wasn't a compliment. You're as stubborn as I am."

"Yes, but I have the manipulative genius of Mom. So I'm golden."

"I love you, Tyler."

"Yeah, I love you, too, Dad."

"I'm going to be okay, you know."

"Uh, yeah. I know."

Top Ten Reasons
Why Keith Richards Is Still Truckin'
and My Dad Is Sick

1. If there is a God, He is an asshole.

2. Fuck off, Keith.

· 13 ·

You Can Take It with You

My father is dead. One day he is there, sitting up, talking to me about car insurance and later that day he is in the morgue. I am numb. It isn't real. People hug me who I have never met in my life and Jell-O is all over the house and I cannot see any reason why gelatin should be the official corpse dessert, but I guess it's as good as macaroni salad or anything else with mayonnaise in it. It all jiggles and looks disgusting and remains half-eaten in the fridge until someone has the guts to pitch it.

I watched my father die. That is the only thing I can remember right now. I should have never tried to get a fucking job again. I should have sponged off my parents forever. At least then I wouldn't have seen him breathing one second, and the next second not breathing. You have no idea what it's like to watch someone die. It is like watching a nuclear bomb go off and seeing people evaporate in front of you. He just ceased to be. I should have never gotten that fucking job.

It had been two months, two full months to the day since I left David and California and all the madness. I was still reeling. But I was also broke. I was at the staffing agency. I was listening to this woman who was supposed to be like my parole officer, even though she was taking fifteen percent of my paycheck to find me a job, so she was more like a parole officer I paid to reprimand me. She was telling me that there was an opening for an emergency room position at Baptist Hospital. All I had to do was accept patients. Write their info in the computer. Get vital information and then leave them to wait or die or whatever. And I was thinking how fun that would be, about as fun as watching my hand catch on fire and burn until there was nothing left but a stub. And then I was thinking that I had to get some money together because I needed to move the hell out of my parents' house even if my dad was getting much worse and I felt guilty about wanting to leave him now, but I was fucking miserable and I needed to get my own space and I had spent all of my savings on my trip to L.A. to see David, and after two months it was clear he never wanted to see me again. So I took the job.

I went through some basic training, and watched other unqualified people enter in the wrong names under the wrong insurance companies, and figured I could manage to almost fuck it up as well as they had, and after a few days I didn't want to stab myself with the letter opener on my tiny desk quite as much. I didn't see the rivers of blood I had expected, but I did see an awful lot of old people who wet their pants when they fell and broke their hips, and I thanked God that I did not have to actually touch the patients. I thought of David at my desk only about ten times an hour, which was an improvement from the last few weeks I had been unemployed. I thought about quitting about one hundred times an hour. That number increased daily.

When my mom came into the ER that Tuesday afternoon, I guess I thought she was bringing me a sandwich or something because I literally acted like this was a normal occurrence. I said "Hi, Mom" and stood up. The white look on her face coupled with the tears on her cheeks didn't quite register until the nurses were running out to the car parked in front of the door. My father was wheeled in, and I watched as these medical students and unfamiliar doctors tried to revive him, and I watched as they called the time of his death, and I watched as they put the sheet over him. And no one ever showed me out of the room like they do on TV and no one said they were sorry, and no one noticed that I wasn't at my post at the front desk admissions and that instead they were paying me $9.75 an hour to watch my father die. And no one noticed when I walked out and never came back.

Top Ten Things
That Suck About Funerals

1. Black is depressing. It makes everyone look about ten shades whiter than they are. We all end up looking like Edward Gorey illustrations.

2. Having a service in a church means they automatically have to talk about God's hand in the death. Explain God's hand in the donations pile. Don't talk about how God thought it would be okay to kill my dad.

3. People cry, especially people who hardly knew my dad, and I want to go up to them and tell them to shut the fuck up, but instead I have to mourn with grace, whatever that means.

4. Let's face it, the music usually sucks. No matter whose funeral you go to.

5. Bible passages, blah blah blah. I don't see how this makes anyone feel comforted.

6. People bring babies to these things. Babies who cry. Because babies don't want to sit there while everyone is thinking about someone who is already dead. So then mothers try to shut the babies up and make more noise in the process and I am thinking that although I would like very much not to have to be here, I would like more for the baby and the mother not to be here.

7. I get hugged by people who tell me my dad was a good man. If they thought he was a good man, they should have told him while he was alive.

8. I also get hugged by people who start crying when they hug me and won't let go of me, and I feel like I have to comfort them, when I'm the one who should be crying and it makes me feel like once again someone else is stealing the moment.

9. My mom does not deal well with deaths in movies. She cries for hours afterward and talks about it like she lost a dear friend. Now imagine how she deals with death in real life.

10. Dad's dead. And he's never coming back.

· 14 ·

Make Me Proud

So we, the Tracer family, now minus one, are in the living room still in our funeral attire. We're supposed to be mourning, I think. Everyone just looks tired. Relieved, somehow. We knew it was coming, thank God at least it's over with. Who's dying next? Who do we give our attention to now?

Mom has a mission she is on. She is holding something for each of us. She holds these white envelopes in her hand like water for children in Ethiopia. Everyone gets one with their name, written in that pressed, dark black ink my father preferred, passed around to them; my older sister Ferris, who has been in denial mode for the entire duration of my father's sickness, and my little sister Judy, who has taken on the role of resident basket case and guilt-ridden child that we have all played at one time or another, my brother, Ray, who I assume could have cared less what was happening to my dad the whole time except that Dad was his fucking financial borrowing institution, so he was pissed that was no longer an option. We all got letters from Dad.

Judy immediately looks over at Ferris's letter and sees that hers is a little longer and starts bawling, instead of actually paying attention to what hers says, and Ray first looks underneath the letter to see if there's any cash in the envelope, which there's not. And I leave the room and take my letter downstairs to the porch swing outside. I don't want to have to perform for them anymore. I don't want to show them how or if this is affecting me at all. When you have siblings, there will always be the invisible stick we all measure with. How much more do you love me, Dad? How much more will you give me? How much more will I put you through? How many more times will you forgive me? But my relationship with my dad is mine, and will never be theirs. I don't care if he wrote he loved them best in theirs, because I had my own issues with my father and we had a stronger bond because of it. I could have never loved my father as much as I did if I hadn't hated him when I was younger. I open the envelope. I am somewhat surprised to see a short note:

Tyler—I found this. Well, what's stopping you?

And then below it, a list of mine my father found. A list that says, "Top Ten Things I Want to Do in Life." The original list. The one I started when I started all this list-making business. This was my father's good-bye to me. A challenge. A little inspiration, a little competition.

My father and I both had artistic temperaments. He knew this even when I was young. Even when he didn't see me all that much. And once I got a little older and we buried hatchets, we would talk for hours about ideas and art and music. And we were always trying to give each other our angles, and competing with each other all along. Rickie Lee Jones will always be more vital than Tori Amos to my father and it was challenging for me to see if I could get him to understand why I related more to Tori, even though I didn't know if I really did. I was trying to give him my perspective, and he was trying to give me his. And sometimes we understood the other's, but we never truly saw it as much as we empathized. We recognized the passion in the perspective and shared that instead. So Dad knew that my lists were my lifeblood. They kept me going as much as my writing did. They still do. And he knew that to give me this list, to give me the words I wrote down, the wishes I had made and maybe forgotten, was to give me more than he could have with a letter about watching me grow up, or about being sorry he was not there anymore. It's a wonderful gift, and at the same time I hate him for giving it to me. Because now I have to do it. I have no choice.

Part III

. . .

The List

· 15 ·

Cat's in the Cradle

"Perry?"

"Yeah?"

"Hey."

"Hey, Tyler."

"Um, hey."

"Yeah."

"Look . . . um, what the hell happened last night?"

"I'm glad you see it that way, too."

"I can't remember anything."

"What the fuck are you talking about?"

"From about the piano on I can't remember shit. I woke up naked on a Hide-a-Bed this morning in your fucking guest room and your mom was tiptoeing out in curlers and a robe. I go from singing Sarah McLachlan at the piano last night with you to being naked in your guest room. Fill me in."

"Uh, well, we were drunk."

"Quite aware of that one, Perry. I drank a fifth of vodka. I'm still drunk. I smell like a fucking distillery twelve hours later. But did we, I mean, did we . . ."

"Yeah. Yeah, we did."

"Oh my God. Oh my God oh my God oh my God. This has never happened to me before. I can't remember anything. I can't remember a goddamn thing! We did not. Ohmygodohmygodohmygod . . ."

"Yeah. If it helps any, it sounded like you were enjoying it. You were screaming and talking dirty, and all."

"Perry, I can't remember being near you. How could I remember enjoying it? Jesus Christ. I slept with you. Oh my God. Did I leave my thong there?"

"I got it."

"Why does my back hurt?"

"It wasn't nice, making-love sort of sex. It was pretty . . . rough."

"But I have a bruise the size of a saucer on my back and my tailbone hurts."

"Tyler, you had your legs above your head at one point. I was pretty impressed."

"Oh my God. Look, did you . . . I mean, did we . . . ?"

"You told me you were on the pill."

"No I did not!"

"Yeah, you told me a couple of times you were on the pill. So I . . . yeah, I would have never done that if I had known."

"Oh fuck."

"Look, everything's cool here. Just take care of that birth control thing, you know. Don't they have RU-486 now?"

"Yeah, Perry. I'll deal with that."

"I don't want to be a daddy. Maybe when I'm in law school, or something."

"Don't even fucking joke about that, Perry. Jesus Christ. No one has ever come inside me. I mean, I never even think about anyone except David at all."

"We were flirting pretty hard-core on the porch. I think that's when it happened."

"No, I remember being on the porch. We talked about . . ."

"Coldplay. That song called 'Science.'"

"No, no, 'The Scientist.' Perry, I wasn't flirting with you then. I wanted to send that song to David in a cheesy high school move. It was the song I wanted to make him think of me . . . kind of. Anyway, I wasn't flirting. I was talking forlornly about him."

"I wanted to do it again but you were passed out and making puking noises."

"Wait, I was passed out? When the fuck did I pass out, Perry?"

"Right after I finished."

"Are you sure?"

"Yeah. You were showing all the signs of major regurgitation so I turned you on your side and went to my bed."

"I didn't throw up."

"Well, you sounded like you were going to."

"I don't remember any of this. I am so fucking upset."

"Look, it's all cool here. Just get those pills or whatever."

"I will *get* the pills. I gotta go. I'll call you when I'm feeling alive. I need to get my thong back before you leave to go back to school."

"Yeah, sure."

"Bye."

I hang up the phone, lying on my sister's bed, in my blue-flannel pajamas, mortified. My pajama bottoms are on backward, because I was drunk when I stumbled home at eight o'clock this morning and I couldn't find my thong in the Hide-a-Bed and I just wanted to get the fuck out of Perry's house and away from his ever-so-nice mother, so I stumbled out and now I don't have any panties on, either. I smell like smoked oysters. My whole body smells like one big smoked oyster and dirty, meaningless, drunk sex. I feel more guilty right now than I did when I lost my virginity to that guy just because I was too fucking weak to say, "No, I have a line and you are crossing it." I sort of feel like I'm standing outside a house and looking inside at a lost, confused girl who does all the wrong things with all the wrong people and then whines about it and never ever learns from it. I sort of feel like I've been taken advantage of and I can't remember enough to call the perpetrator on his shit.

Last night, I'll admit I was running away from my problems. I'm trying to deal with my dead father and his challenge and I don't know how, and grief is not a word that I recognize as a healthy process for some reason, and I'm truly pissed off that I can't even call David and tell him my father is dead because he doesn't care. He manages to come off as this terribly kind person, but he would turn a deaf ear to a woman running screaming out of a burning building just to avoid confrontation. So obviously, I haven't told him about my dad.

Perry had just come into town from school last night when he called, and even though he might not have cared as much as he sounded, I needed to hear something besides silence. Perry and I got to know each other about a year back when he wanted to be a songwriter and I wanted to be anything but what I was and we tried to date, but there was absolutely nothing whatsoever between us at all from the get-go. So we were drinking buddies. We used to go to the Sunset Grille after his songwriters' showcases after midnight and eat overpriced pasta and drink kamikazes and talk about all the shit we were going to do when we got our lives together. Perry sort of felt out the Nashville music scene for a few months and realized it was muddier than he once thought. Some people try to write a hit for their whole lives and die in Nashville working at Tootsie's for tips. Or they sell out and write country music. I guess Perry decided law was a better route, maybe a little more honest. Seriously, it probably is. So he went back to school to finish up there, and back to his girlfriend, who he never really left anyway. She's a real piece of work. I still don't know why, although I imagine Perry wanted her to believe it, but she actually thought Perry and I were sleeping together and she came at me at a party once, like some total cracked-out white trash girl on *Jerry Springer*. That proved to be a bit of a deterrent to Perry and my hanging out together much, especially since he was at school down South again, and I like the part of the South he was in about as much as I like having a recurring nightmare. Nothing against the South in general, because I am Southern, I just happen to think people of color and women deserve as much respect as drunk, overprivileged, stupid, southern white men. So I've always had an issue with about eighty percent of the student population at a lot of Southern universities.

So Perry and I have been trying to keep in touch ever since his psychotic girlfriend dumped him and ever since I got involved with David. He was interested in why I was so interested in another musician and not him, and although I cared about Perry's situation with this psycho girl he had an entanglement with, I knew also that Perry is a good listener, and I had exhausted my supply of kind, patient ears in the Nashville vicinity. So when he came back into town, I was really glad to hear from him. I think we both knew we would need someone to cry to about all of it.

On the way to Perry's, I stopped by my favorite old haunt of yesteryear, the old liquor store down the road, the one I went to nightly about a year back with these "friends" I once had who are, to this day, the epitome of what you would call total fucking alcoholics. I still see one or two of them on random and infrequent visits to bars and they're still all the same. Drunk. Rude. Throwing up on themselves or someone next to them. Cheating on their girlfriends, who have now become their wives, or ex-wives already. Hitting on me. It makes me never want to date anyone who drinks, who has a dick . . . who has a pulse.

Every time I go to that liquor store now, it's a special occasion. And every time I walk in, I see the same guy I know because of my past visits, and every time I wonder why I'm in there again when I'd really rather be at home playing rummy and drinking hot tea. But I always manage to talk myself into the drink. It always finds its way in somehow.

I think that there are two types of alcoholics. People who would mainline Jack if it got them fucked-up faster, the people who lie to drink, who hide their drinking, who wake up vomiting but still end up pouring bourbon into the coffee an hour later, people who will drink anything even if it's not meant to be a beverage to get the alcohol content into their systems . . . the desperate ones. And then there's another type. The ones who are on the path. Who have the illusion of control, but also a family history that looks like the Kennedys. People who have grown up knowing the smell of liquor, and have learned to associate it with guilt and shame and lies and disappointment from their elders. People who see alcoholism as most people see the Holocaust. A terrible tragedy. One that has affected us, and continues to take the lives of people we love. People who still have a drink with everyone else even when they see all the horrors a drink can create. People like me.

You see, when I walked into Perry's house with the vodka in my little brown paper bag, when I played pool and got better as I got drunker, when I decided to keep tossing down those drinks that had about five shots of vodka to a jigger of 7 UP even after I started faltering a little, I was doing something underhanded. I was getting back at Dad, who gave me the thirst that can never be quenched and who left me too soon. I was getting back at David, who wouldn't fucking say good-bye. I was hurting myself and saying, "Look how deep this wound is! I'm bleeding to death! What will you do now?" And they both answered when I woke up this morning, naked, shamed: Nothing.

At first, it was all very casual. I wore my burnt sienna suede pants last night because I had bought them for my trip to see David, and had never gotten a chance to wear them in California. I had all these adorable fashion plate items stowed away in my suitcase while I was with David that would never be released because he wore the same thing every day for a week, and made me feel self-conscious when I changed once a day. So I never wore the things I had chosen especially for him, especially for nights out on the town that never happened, especially to convince him that I was intelligent *and* I knew my way around a fashion house. I tried to dumb down my clothes so I didn't feel like a prima donna around him. All the cute outfits now hung in my closet like lovers tossed aside. They cried to be noticed. They still had price tags on them.

So anyway, I had these suede pants. These soft-as-butter beautiful suede pants that I bought on a whim right after David and I began talking and I decided that I was going to go and see him someday once upon a time. I was morally opposed to suede, and I still am, to be honest, but they were the symbol of this new life, a life where things were not constantly weighed with consequences, where maybe I could wear leather boots and not be a Nazi, where those suede pants could be worn and pulled off of me one lusty night in the future by a charming guy in California who I had a crush on. With every outfit I bought, I had a night and an adventure planned. So I grabbed the pants off their hanger last night and, in an act of bitter revenge, I wore them to Perry's house for the first time ever. Just to see if David would notice from two thousand miles away.

Perry was casual and shabby, having just arrived from his road trip from school. He seemed nervous. It was weird. Perry hadn't been nervous around me since we first decided that dating was something he and I should never do together. But he acted like I was a first date all of a sudden, and it made me nervous, too. I felt like I had to make polite conversation and comment on the boring prints on the wall so we wouldn't be faced with silence. I should have known then that things were not quite right.

We drank red wine first. It was shitty red wine, and the only reason I knew this was probably because David knows all about wines of every kind, and I had a few really decent California reds while I was with him. Pinot Noirs and Cabernets and Merlots with names I had never heard, in deep green bottles that always looked pretty the next day, emptied out, with flowers in them in the window above the kitchen sink. David used to sniff at the corks in the grocery store before he put them in the cart, and he only bought reds, which I was always against before I met David simply because that was the drink of choice for my dad and the smell and color of Merlot brought back bad memories. But I was just excited to feel like a grown-up, buying wine at the store and planning meals and such, and I got into the process. So all of a sudden, I fancied myself a wine connoisseur, and I decided this wine Perry offered up was shitty stuff. But I gulped it. No sipping last night. I gulped and talked as I gulped.

We got out pool cues and started playing pool, and I gig-
gled a little too much, but I was trying on that careless, happy
personality I never have been good at when my life is falling
apart. Perry couldn't find orange juice, so he tried to squeeze
oranges until he realized we wanted to start drinking within
this century, so we settled for mixing the vodka with 7 UP left
over in the pantry. It tasted like nothing, really. When you're in
the mind-set I've been in, I think you could drink motor oil for
effect and it would taste like water. I was concentrating on the
feeling, not the taste. I wanted feeling back, and if I couldn't
feel love from David or a presence from my father, I would
replace that feeling with this one. Dizzy giddiness.

Two wines and two steep vodkas and two conversation-
filled pool games later, Perry brought out crackers and smoked
oysters. I remember the smell of them as he opened the can,
like raw sewage and smelly underwear three days old, and it
still makes me retch. I looked at him with amused disgust, asking as I took a whiff close up how on earth he could ever eat
anything that smelled like that. Perry said, "Well, I've been eating pussy for ten years, so . . ." And I remember thinking that
he must date girls who don't take showers very often because
this smell was not what I was reminded of when I thought of
my own sexual secretions. I always thought I smelled of cream
cheese. Of vanilla oil and a nice cream cheese. And come always
smells like metallic buttermilk to me. And tastes a bit like
mucus. But this smell was just obscene. I should have known I
was getting knee-walking-rowdy drunk when I volunteered to
taste one of these gray squiggly things that looked like road-

kill. I hadn't eaten anything dead in seven years. But I kept going. I chewed the disgusting, slimy, sewage-smelling thing and it tasted worse than it smelled, and right then I knew that I had become, in the last three months, someone I don't like very much. So I kept drinking. And talking.

Perry was pulling out all the stops. All I talked about the entire time revolved around David. How brilliant he was, how funny he was, how talented, how good the sex was, how much I missed him. . . . This was the ultimate night of dedication to David. And each time I mentioned something David did that I loved, I guess Perry was subconsciously taking notes. When I told him about the night David played his music for me, the night I realized how deep this all went, Perry pushed it aside, and then twenty minutes later we were in the library singing covers of Big Star and Carly Simon, Perry playing on the guitar, me singing my drunk little heart out. I think he had been trying to show me that he was just like David all night. I think he thought he would be a good substitute. We're both over-dramatic, and overly romantic. But I was drunk, and I was sure I was sending the same message I had been ever since David had entered my consciousness: I am in love with some-one no one could ever be. Don't even try it. Not even the object of my affections can live up to what I've made him to be. So I thought I was safe.

The last clear memory I have is of singing "Possession" with Perry and flubbing the words, and then picking up my pool cue. We listened to the Waterboys. We talked more about relationships. And from there, nothing. Not even a moment where I remember a smell, a feel, a word. Perry says I flirted with him. He says I was an animal, that I enjoyed it. That makes me more ill than anything else does, I suppose, because I haven't even had a thought of anyone besides David since I've known him. I never wanted to lust after anyone like I lusted after him. I might have been passed out, and even if I wasn't, obviously it wasn't so good I care to remember anything specific. And anyway, I never enjoyed sex with David. I needed it. I screamed and begged him to do it to me over and over just like a battered woman returns to her assailant. I always screamed because he was filling this hole I could never fill completely on my own, and I knew that he would empty it again soon and I would be left all alone.

I am all alone now, and I have come to grips with the fact that I could have a drinking problem. At the very least I am at risk. And this is the first thing I will accomplish. When I open the list Dad gave me and look down at number ten, the one I must have written when I was about seventeen, after the first time I had ever been drunk in my life, when I passed out in my front yard and puked for two days straight. I resolve to end this fatal dance. I mark through the item after number ten that says, "Stop drinking."

Top Ten Best Things About Alcohol

1. Buzzes. No one tells you when you're young, when they're preaching to just say no and all that bullshit, that buzzes feel so fuzzy and nice and warm. It is possible to just drink for that buzz and keep it going all night long if you gauge it just right. I think the reason people get shitfaced most of the time is that they can't gauge their tolerance worth a shit and they're trying to keep that buzzed feeling all night. Buzzes are like two hours of oral sex. They're relaxing. Soft. Ticklish almost.

2. Alcohol gives shy guys balls. This can be good if the guy is your type and murder if he's not.

3. Alcohol lowers your inhibitions. So being naked, even when you feel bloated and disgusting and you've eaten about a million peanuts and pretzels at the bar, seems like a perfectly natural thing to do.

4. Alcohol gives a huge segment of the population something to do. We are a bored species. We figure out tons of ways to make things easier for ourselves, giving us way too much free time, so we have to get drunk to pass the time we've saved by busting our asses to save time.

5. Alcohol is the world's greatest excuse. "Did I say I thought you were a nasty bitch? Oh, I must have been drunk." "Did I say I loved you? I was drunk." "Did I really say I liked to listen to old Debbie Gibson songs? I was drunk. I must have been drunk."

6. Face it. Half of us would not be on this planet if our parents hadn't been drunk.

7. Alcohol can taste good. Especially when it has all that shit mixed in. Bitters and vermouth and cherries and sugar and soda and Grand Marnier and Triple Sec and ice. It's all about the girl drinks. They're the secret to letting booze grow on you. I still taste a perfect Long Island iced tea in my sleep.

8. Alcohol is cool. I don't care who you are, if you're drinking a martini, you're suddenly ten shades cooler. The phrase "No thanks, I don't drink" will never be considered cool, especially to social people, because "social people" is a nice way of saying drunkards.

9. Alcohol makes everything funny. Everything. Yes, that's why you laughed when the cops pulled you over and when they wanted to take you into jail for DUI, you called shotgun, and it was so fucking funny. It wasn't so funny the next day when you were sober in jail, was it?

10. Alcohol is a way of life. People build wine cellars, they toast their wedding days with champagne, they drink at funerals, they form whole memories around booze. And sometimes I feel like I'll never have fun again without it.

· 16 ·

Driving Under Influences

"DoubleuKayAr-emm! The only station that plays continuous music all the time . . . no talk, no pop, only continuous hits while you listen. We are the only station that rocks your area. No talk, just ro . . ."

A whole lot of radio stations talk for hours about how they don't talk. I click the radio off and pop in a CD I made before I left. Howie Day fills the car with his raspy butter voice singing "Ghost." I light a Marlboro and toss out the burned-out match as I roll the windows down in Dad's old '79 orange Mercedes convertible. The top is already down. The wind whips around me and makes it hard to hear the music unless I turn it all the way up. So that's what I do. I pass eighteen wheelers and minivans with families in them on Interstate 40. I pass tour buses every other minute with horses and flags airbrushed on the backs. I drive faster when the chorus hits. I sing along as my reddish-blondish hair flies all over the place and look for my turn through my dark metal sunglasses I bought at the Dallas–Ft. Worth airport when I went to see David. I'm taking off.

Nashville is the place I was born. Right downtown by the Krispy Kreme and Elliston Place Soda Shop at Baptist Hospital. I can drive around my big city in the country and in every part of town, I have a place I can point to where something happened that changed my life. Bellevue, where I lived in that little apartment with Mom and Dad and Ferris before Judy was born, where Ferris almost drowned in the duck pond and I learned to swim in the little aquamarine swimming pool. Before the big mall there was built, before Bon Jovi made it safe for mallrats to backcomb their permed hair and move to places like Bellevue, where they would be protected from trends and modern advances in salon equipment. Linton, that little place we moved once Mom had Judy. I grew up in that ranch-style house past the Loveless Motel, past the gas station where that woman was hit by a car when she checked her mail. The country, the real country, with crawdaddies in the front yard and a donkey and a cow and barbed wire fences and pine trees and creeks and the Harpeth River keeping us safe from real civilization and real neighbors. The place my mother hated, the place we kids needed, the hills and woods to hide and pretend in, the blackberry bushes to feed us when the summer sun was so hot and the house was too far away to walk back to. The place I learned to say "y'all" and "shitfire" with conviction. Forest Hills, where we moved once I turned sixteen and learned how to drive in the real Nashville, the city part, where all my friends had always lived. The hills and the traffic competing with the deer that came out of the woods and would always end up limp and lifeless on the side of Harding Place. Downtown, where I would go as a young teenager into all the old antique shops that used to line Second Avenue, and then were replaced by trendy martini bars and country music souvenir shops and Planet Hollywood and Hard Rock Café. Downtown, where I used to go to the Italian street fair every year and get my palm read, the fortune-teller, the seer, always saying the same things to me, that I would never have to worry about money, that my true love was far, far away, that I was born an old woman and I would be getting younger as I get older. And I believed her, every year, I believed her. The same place we all did our pub crawls when I got older, where I passed out at Jack Legs after Sage had dumped me and I was depressed enough to convince myself that a couple more tequila shots would make everything much better. The hospital over off West End that my friend George took me the same night just to make sure I wasn't going to die of alcohol poisoning. The same hospital Mom and Dad took me to every time I had jumped off something else and cracked something else open. Belle Meade, fancy-schmancy Belle Meade with its millionaires and poor little rich wives with their SUVs and their Valium and their sons who courted girls like me when I went to that all-girls school, and then broke the hearts of girls like me because I didn't exude the right Belle Meade flair. Sylvan Park, where we used to go for cornbread at Bro's and then later where that jerk who had the wife lived, the first and certainly not the last bastard who tried to turn me into the mistress that I refused to be. All these parts of town I know by heart, even though I still sometimes get lost on their side streets, every once and again. I am leaving all of this. I am going to conquer this list. Mark Knopfler's "Long Highway" comes on. Damn, I'm good at this mixed driving music thing. I should be the DJ at "doubleuKayArr-emm." As I pull on to 40 and out of the city, I take out my list and cross out number seven, "Get out of Nashville."

Top Ten Best Driving Songs

1. "Running Down a Dream"—Tom Petty: No explanation needed. This has got to be the cause of about twenty-five percent of the speeding tickets on highways everywhere.

2. "The Breakup Song"—the Greg Kihn Band: I mean, especially in light of my recent events, this is fucking killer. You have to drum your palms on the steering wheel to the beat. It's the rule.

3. "Goddess on a Hiway"—Mercury Rev: I think this is actually about morphine and the lead singer doing morphine with some junkie chick or the drug itself being a goddess or something. Whatever. All I know is that when this song comes on, I roll down my windows, let the wind whip all around me, and try to imagine myself in this movie in my head where the cherry of my spent cigarette hits the pavement at the exact same moment the chorus begins, and the hot ash explodes behind my car in all sorts of tiny fireworks.

4. "I Know There's Something Going On"—Frida: The first time I heard this song was way, way past its heyday. I was in a limo doing lines of coke off of CD cases and rolling on X and drinking champagne on a crazy New Year's night in Nashville a few years back with a bunch of shady people I knew. It was freezing but the E's were making us warm so we had the windows rolled down and we were all raising our hands and beating the air to the chorus of this song, while the limo swerved and took us to another location to find more drugs, or cham-

pagne, I can't remember which. I kept thinking, This song should have been huge, even though I think it already was once upon a time when I was about eight. But nevertheless, I can still drive very fast and recklessly to this song and almost feel like I'm being as careless and young and stupid as I was that night.

5. "Power of Two"—Indigo Girls: I know, I'm cheesy and girly and all that, but this reminds me of the way a relationship should be. You jump in the beat-up old convertible with your guy, with a couple pairs of jeans, a pair of boots, a few T-shirts, and a bunch of tunes and you just take off, resting your head on his shoulder while you drive down lone country roads just getting lost and eating Cheetos and truck stop sandwiches. That's romance.

6. "Digging in the Dirt"—Peter Gabriel: Peter must do a lot of driving because he always manages to incorporate the rhythm of a moving car into his songs. Especially a great song if you're driving in the South, where there are trees and kudzu all over the sides of the roads that seem to grow and crawl around next to you as you speed by.

7. "Better"—Modlang: Movie in my head, part two. The top's down, the wind's blowing, the sun is setting all orange and pink in the distance, and for one moment, one actual moment in time on some unimportant highway in some unimportant place, I am feeling secure with some small portion of my life. Sometimes I think it's actually enough to hear pretty sounds and distorted

guitars and complicated but beautifully simple melodies like this and not think, just listen.

8. "The Ballad of Resurrection Joe (Ilsa She-Wolf of Hollywood Mix)"—Rob Zombie: This song is the L.A. freeway. It is death and destruction and dirt and smog and sex and traffic and all that comes with it. I listened to this song about ten times when I was driving around L.A. for the first time a few years back. It just suits the drive, the road conditions, everything. It's like Satan singing a Volkswagen commercial or something. Like when I first heard that James song on the cold and flu medicine commercial. It worked. It seemed cheesy, but it works.

9. "Gimme Shelter"—Rolling Stones: I still think the Stones were like the ultimate futuristic band. They did everything first. But just because Mick's lips were so luscious and Keith was such a fucking druggie, it took the attention from the fact that they wrote stellar music. The tinny guitar in this, the percussion that sounds like someone running their fingernails over a comb, just the whole vibe is dark and the perfect segue for some sort of driving scene in a movie. The Stones rock. Sorry, Keith. No offense to you earlier. I just miss Dad.

10. "Torn"—Edna Swap: It's just low-key and acoustic but longing, and I listened to the acoustic version of this song once when I was on a little highway on the way to a friend's lake house and we were stoned and the day seemed so long and we needed to chill out and this song

came through for us. This song makes me feel like she's saying what I've always wanted to say. That girls have these things, these seeds that are planted in us, these nurturing seeds and wanting seeds and romance seeds and sensitive, human emotion seeds and we will always feel a little rejected because men are not gardeners.

· 17 ·

Another One Bites the Dust

Listening to Dusty Springfield and smoking the last ciga-rette in my pack. I'm going to have to stop within the next twenty minutes to get some more cigs and a Dr Pepper or things might get ugly. You have to chain-smoke and listen to Dusty and drink sugary, fizzly long-necked Dr Peppers when you're in Memphis. It's a rite of passage, like the dirty streets, the ghost town of a downtown, the Mississippi River that gave us industry and took Jeff Buckley as collateral. Memphis is the town of promise, a place that could be great if things hadn't gone the way they did, if it wasn't so close to other places in Tennessee that caused friction, like Pulaski. Memphis oozes this desire to be more than the home of Beale Street and Elvis and the Peabody Hotel, where the ducks are led down to the fountain every morning and led back up to the cage the Peabody calls their penthouse in the evening. As I drive along the bumpy, pothole-filled streets of downtown, I decide that I am going to hit the town of Memphis tonight, and maybe even go to Rendezvous Ribs, even if I can't eat the meat, just for atmosphere. But first, I have to find a motel. A cheap motel that won't dent the two thousand bucks I have from the account Dad left for me. It wasn't much, and I have to spend it wisely. I find a little yellow motel that says on the sign above free cable, swimming pool and pull in there. I don't have a swimsuit, but kicking back on cheap sheets and watching crappy cable TV doesn't sound so bad . . . maybe I'll go swimming in my shorts later.

I walk into the main office that smells a bit like vomit and chlorine, and the lady with the thickest bifocals I've ever seen is watching a little TV and eyeing me suspiciously.

"We don't give student discounts."

"I'm not a student."

"The pool's closed . . . for repairs." I look through the window at a muddy hole in the ground that surely must never have enclosed a real pool, maybe a reservoir of bubonic plague or something when this motel was first built, but never a clear blue-tiled pool where people swam.

"And the cable's . . . out." I'd venture to say it never was "in" in the first place, but I don't care. I'm exhausted and I just want a place to rest.

For thirty-nine bucks, I have my own room with brown shag carpet, a lime green poly-cotton-blend comforter that I will remove immediately, a TV, a painting of a barn and two cows, and a piece of soap maybe the size of my thumb. I think towels must be extra, but I brought my own anyway. The lady also had cigarettes for sale at the counter. Big plus. They were marked up about two bucks and she only had Marlboro Reds, but I got them anyway. Lungs, this is going to be a long night. I throw one of the bags on the floor of my room, slip my boots off, and literally pass out on the bed the minute I hit it. That drive from Nashville to Memphis is historically the most boring, draining ride ever. So I sleep. And dream of Elvis. And of David when things were good.

When I wake up, it's to the sounds of a game show or a porn movie, I can't tell which, playing in the next room. And a commode flushing. I have fallen asleep face down with my sunglasses on and they have left a pinkish bruise on the bridge of my nose. I forgot to take the comforter off, and I have seen enough local news exposés to know that these things are worse than licking toilet seats as far as germs go. So as I turn my head and notice a smell I can only describe as metallic buttermilk, and recognizing the most likely source of that smell, I sit up quickly and rip the comforter off the bed.

What is it about waking up after a nap that makes me suicidal? I always wake up and feel like I've slacked off, like I'm not supposed to be asleep at that time, that the divine master plan does not include me napping from 4:00 P.M. until 6:30 P.M. and that I was supposed to accomplish my greatness in that time frame and I have missed out on the opportunity to be a legend. And then I remember that I don't believe in a master plan, except maybe when it comes to disappointment. When in doubt, trust it won't work out.

I had promised myself earlier I was going to head out on the town because you can't go on a road trip and not get a piece of the local color to remember. I force myself to put my boots on and light a cigarette as I get up to look in the mirror by the sink. Oh yeah. That pink mark looks cute. And my windblown hair looks even cuter. People with convertibles are not meant to have good hair. But I had to take Dad's old car. He left it to me, and it's romantic, having a convertible on a roadtrip, even if it is noisy and a pain in the ass to shut because it's almost older than me.

I stash my extra cash in a baggie taped under the sink, something my dad always used to do on our summer vacations, and pack my cigarettes, twenty bucks (it's pretty cheap to go out if you don't drink), some lipgloss, and my ID in my little velvet purse, and decide to brush my hair on the way. It's not like I'm actually looking to get picked up or anything anyway. The door to the room slams shut and I decipher that it is indeed a porno playing in the room next to mine, which means the cable must be "out" unless you slip the girl at the front desk a fifty. Even the Lone Oak Motel has politics involved, I guess. The parking lot looks like a place where either hookers hang out or where Selena got shot in the back, so I kind of feel bad when I climb in to Dad's old car and realize I left it unlocked. But who would rob an orange Mercedes anyway?

I pull out of the parking lot and turn on the CD player again. "Woman" by John Lennon is on. It's too bad Yoko Ono has anything to do with this song or it might make me feel all warm and romantic and fuzzy. I find my way back downtown and park by a meter that already has two hours paid on it, and try to appear poised and confident as I stride down an alley all by myself because that's what I've read might make a rapist not want to rape me as much, even though I think if I were a rapist I would avoid the pathetic victim-type people because confident people turn me on much more anyway. This club, the Mole Hole, has blues emanating from it, and you can't do Memphis without blues, so I decide it's the place I'm going to try first. I walk in and the big bouncer with gold teeth and cornrows asks me how old I am. I feel very small and glad that I'm not underage as I nearly whisper "twenty-four" and walk on past as he smiles. This place is slammed. No seats, no room for moving. The last band is just leaving the stage and about a million people try to hit the bar all at once. I somehow make it to the space over by the bathrooms and watch as an old black man walks up to the stage and sits down at the piano. Everyone's talking while he starts to play. A cocktail waitress walks by with a tray of some of the most beautiful drinks I've ever seen. Tom Collinses and margaritas and hurricanes, all with cherries and limes, ice cubes clinking around the glasses. This is what I already miss about drinking. Pretty colors and pretty glasses and being treated well by the waitress instead of having tap water handed to me in a paper cup like this girl just did on her way to paying customers. But the good thing about blues clubs is that they're smoky, so I can smoke and satisfy my oral fixation in that way. Pretend I have something to do with my hands. I listen for a while to the blues this old man plays, over the din of a bunch of suburban white cocktail drinkers, while he drinks gin. Straight gin. Just like a bootlegger back in the day.

I look around at the crowd, at guys trying to gauge just how close they are to bedding their dates, at couples who have been together for a while and use liquor and music to convince themselves they still have a good time with one another. I think about all the reasons I hate this kind of life, dashing off after work to some date that I dress up for, only to realize half into it that if I don't get drunk, I'll be bored out of my mind. I think about how for the most part it's not just drinking that makes things seem better. It's ambiance. Clubs and restaurants and movie theaters and hell, even church are just dressed-up forms of reality. You go to a restaurant to make eating seem like an activity, an event, a sensuous night out. You go to bars to turn beverages into a way to pass time, a way to meet people. You go to church to make the process of trying to figure out what you're doing here and why life is so fucking hard some kind of a ceremonious event, when really it's just going on Sunday to a building you ended up paying for to talk to someone who might not be there, and pretend he's talking back. And I hate this sort of delay of reality. Even this blues club. The music is nice and all, but I would rather be driving and find my own blues station on the radio. At least then I don't feel stagnant. At least then I'm still moving. I put my cigarette out in my water and wade through the crowd once again, the big bouncer winking at me on the way out. I somehow make it back to my car in that shady alley without being raped, and turn on my radio, trying to find a cool blues station on the way back to the motel. All I can find are top forty and country stations. Figures. Even Memphis can't escape the plague of bad radio. I pull into the Lone Oak Motel again and park directly in front of my door, finding my key at the bottom of my little velvet purse and being greeted again, as I walk in, by the smell of disinfectant lightly overlaying the smells of vomit, wet carpet, and mediocrity. I feel as if I'm drunk by proxy of those blues club patrons, my eyes heavy and my legs weighted. I pull my jeans off and resolve to sleep in my T-shirt and undies. I don't want to get out anything else. I just want to sleep again. To sleep and pretend this, all of this, the last twenty years, was all a dream.

Sirens wake me up this time. Sirens and the same smell I remember from when I was in third grade when our little house in the country burned down. Soot and fire and smoke and that burned-out sort of chemical-like smell that happens when plastic burns. At first I just sit up and listen. I hear CB radios and boots and some of the other motel doors shutting. There's a bang at my door, followed by a crack. Someone is breaking down the door, and the smoke is now visible as it pours into my room from the parking lot. From the outside light I can see a figure approach me. I am still in bed, just waiting to see what happens next.

"Ma'am? Ma'am, there's a fire in one of the other rooms. You need to come with me." I'm sort of paralyzed. Half-awake. I start to sit up and realize I'm only partly dressed underneath the sheets.

"Can you, like, turn around, or something? I don't have any pants on." The fireman mutters something like "Jesus frickin' Christ" under his breath and turns around as I jump out of bed and slip my jeans and boots on and run over to the sink to get the money underneath. I grab my bag by the bed and follow

145

the figure outside, where everything is more visible. Red lights and a bunch of people in boxers and robes and curlers in their hair, just staring at the front office of the motel, engulfed in flames. I'm watching, too, as I throw my bag into Dad's car and remember something. I start to run back into my room and the fireman who earlier escorted me out stops me in front of the door.

"Ma'am? What do you think you're doing?" He's got a big fireman hat on and soot on his face, but he's fairly young. Too young to be calling me ma'am. It's a Southern thing, I guess. We're all forced to be polite from an early age.

"I . . . forgot something." I'm too embarrassed to tell him what I'm willing to risk life and limb for. I could just buy more cigarettes.

"Well, you're just going to have to live without it."

"What happened . . . I mean, to the lady in there?"

"Lady? Well, that's good to know."

"What do you mean? You didn't know she's in there?"

"Ma'am, all we know is something was in there. But it's BBR at this point."

"BBR?"

"Burnt beyond recognition. Charred. Completely unrecognizable." It comforts me little to hear how nonchalant the fireman is about anyone being "BBR." Or charred, for that matter. I thought for sure there was a note in the fire chief book of etiquette that warned against nicknames for corpses. Next he'll ask if I want a s'more.

"What happened? What was the cause?"

"Well, we're not officially sure yet, but between you and me, I have a pretty good idea. It's a common story. Maybe she was smoking and fell asleep with the cigarette in her mouth. And maybe the hair spray she probably had in her hair, coupled with the incredibly flammable nature of the stuff she was probably drinking. . . . Well, I don't want to be crude, but she probably made nice kindling." Oh my God. Just as the fireman finishes his gruesome account, I can recognize the smell I thought before was plastic. It's burning flesh. Flesh and hair. I can't believe he's deduced all this from so little. How often does this happen really?

"Ma'am? What'd you want out of that room? I might be able to sneak in for you." The fireman gives me a wink. I feel sick to my stomach as I mumble, "Nothing. I don't think I'll need them anymore anyway."

I get in my car and take off for the road. I can't sleep now. As I pull onto the interstate, and crank up Tom Waits's "Clap Hands," I reach over to the passenger side for my list and cross off number six: "Stop smoking."

Top Ten Things
I Swear I Was in a Past Life

1. Leona Carrington, because she was tragic and artistic and overdramatic and she fell in love with an old man who treated her with hardly any regard at all, and she loved him endlessly and sacrificed her entire life basically to serve him. Or so I remember it going that way in the movie . . .

2. An exotic dancer. I don't have the exhibitionist nerve that makes me want to be naked around people, but I have this need to lock myself up every once in a while with some serious strip music and get jiggy with it. I must shake it.

3. A nun. Because my sex drive is huge, and I must have deprived myself for my whole life last time around to want it this much now. Or maybe I would stop thinking about it all the time if I got it once a day. That would be enough for me. I think.

4. A rock star. I just know I was. It's in me. I'm decadent and ridiculous and self-conscious, and every act ends up feeling like people are watching me and taking notes on the secret life of Tyler Tracer, when really no one gives a shit. Plus, I'm obsessed with music. My life is all about music and a little sex and misery. And musicians always end up relating to me. A product of growing up around them. It's a curse.

5. A mommy. Another curse. Every baby in every plane, grocery store, restaurant reaches for me. I am a nurturer out of necessity. It's out of control.

6. A race car driver. I speed like it keeps me alive.

7. A chef. I can be a damn good cook, and even when I fuck things up, I always manage to make one dish that saves the day.

8. A psychologist. I can have anyone I meet figured out in 2.5 seconds. That doesn't mean I ever heed these perceptions, of course.

9. A psychic. Isn't a psychic just an untrained psychologist, though, with a crystal ball?

10. A smoker. Call it intuition. I'm quitting all the things that used to define me. Who will I be now?

· 18 ·

Sensory Deprivation

I take back what I said about Memphis being the most boring drive. The one from Memphis through Little Rock,
Arkansas, is. Especially late at night. It's kind of like boring sex.
It's not all that involved, it's not all that terrible, but it's just
there. Like Matchbox Twenty songs and pink carnations and
Honda Civics and other things you might find on a secretary's
desk or in her driveway. God, I sound like such a snob.

I heard Don Henley on the radio after I pulled out of the
craziness of last night's fire and I started crying. Now either
I'm getting soft or I have that thing people get when they go
through something traumatic, what's it called? Post-traumatic
stress disorder? I dunno. Whatever it is, there's no way I am
now an adult contemporary sucker. It has to be the fire and the
smell of burning flesh and the stress of not smoking in the last
half hour. I mean, crying to "The Heart of the Matter"? Jesus. I
might as well buy all the Meg Ryan videos where she crumples

150

up her nose and puts on that I'm-so-damn-cute-you-just-*have*-to-relate-to-me! look. I might as well watch *Sleepless in Seattle* and eat a pint of ice cream when I'm depressed just because that's stereotypically what I'm supposed to do as a single old maid. Oh my God. I'm twenty-four and I have now surrendered my fate to that end.

I think I had an anxiety attack. I didn't know what they really were before, and believe me, no one wants to know. I always thought people who said they had anxiety attacks were being overdramatic and just total pussies. But I'm serious, I thought I was going to die. I had no desire to stop at another motel just yet in light of recent events, so I decided to keep driving, and I was sort of lost, and I had already bawled at the Don Henley song, and then Color Me Badd came on directly afterward and I realized I was listening to the least cool station on the planet, so I popped in another mix CD and pressed random play and of course Coldplay came on, but this time it was "Clocks" instead of "The Scientist," and it could have actually been "Trouble" coming on, or the most obvious but brilliant one, "Yellow," but it didn't really matter because Coldplay could very well be the best band on the planet and the guy who sings sounds like pain. He is the king of break-up songs and sweet ballads and he sometimes just sings that note that makes my heart jump, the one David played in that song of his that made me have to sort of find my heartbeat again. E flat. Or maybe it was F minor. I dunno. I only made it to two guitar lessons before I decided that anyone who can read or play music is a frickin' genius. I admit that I have a penchant for

British boys in bands, so my thing for Coldplay could also stem from this obsession, but whatever.

The point is, Coldplay came on and I was not crying, I was sobbing, and singing along, and then my sobbing sort of turned into a wailing that nearly flew over the music and the sound of the wind because the top was down again, and it felt like the wind was taking my breath and I couldn't get it back, and I had to stop the car because I had basically started hyperventilating. So I'm on the side of the road, having an anxiety attack, and I really thought I was having a heart attack, and I kept clutching my chest, then my neck, and grabbing on to the seat next to me, as if touching something real would make this terrible thing not real. Then I thought that if I died right there on the way to Little Rock I would just not ever get to die in some villa in the South of France as I had hoped, so I kept thinking, I cannot die. I have to breathe. But I sort of couldn't come to grips with this being anything but a precursor to death as Peter Gabriel's "Here Comes the Flood" came on.

I thought, I'm going to die of a broken heart. David is killing me, he is actually killing me, and if I could describe this dying to him, surely he wouldn't do it. He doesn't mean to hurt me this badly, he doesn't mean to kill me, does he? And then I focused on how I've always dated guys who were sort of mentally unstable and how Sage and Henry and David all had told me about having anxiety attacks before, and I thought they were just being precious.

And I realized that I had actually witnessed David having one of these attacks, and had no idea how truly horrible it was as I

sat there on the bed watching him sort of gasp a little and grab at his chest and get up to hide the magnitude of it from me. I had brushed it off. And now I know that he thought he was dying. David thought he was dying quite often. And I can't imagine how mortified he must have been to feel like he was dying right in front of me and then to realize it was a false alarm. To have such little control over your perception of your own safety is the most unsettling feeling you can imagine. And now I understand it. How could anyone act like a normal person after realizing this could happen at any moment? One time David actually went to the hospital over one of these attacks. And they ran a bunch of tests and then just told him to get over it and sent him home. Can you imagine the humiliation of that?

Mental imbalance is about as acceptable as herpes. It's never going to be accepted. But really, it's a disease, just like cancer. It just happens, and it eats away all the good parts of your brain, like judgment and happiness and perception and memory and life. And you can die from depression like any other disease. And it's not as if people choose it. So why is it still a joke of medicine? "Tyler died of cancer" is a lot more socially acceptable to people than "Tyler committed suicide." Why?

I've had my own battles with the disease, and sometimes I think it might end up winning, but most of the time I just feel really angry that it's a contender at all. My mood. My depression. "The thing." It's not a weakness like my family always told me it was, it's not like having a thing for chocolate or for red shoes. I can't remember actually the first time I was depressed. It might have been at birth. I dunno. Mom always said it was when I got my tonsils out, as if when they opened me up and ripped out some glands, my brain just decided that living was no longer a viable option. She thinks it's all the surgeon's fault for taking out my diseased tonsils, not her fault for passing on her own imbalances that show when she begins to shake and talk through her teeth and drive the car so fast toward the telephone pole that I am sure she really is trying to kill me. Not my father's fault for passing on his brooding, his tendency to get up and make a scene if he's not satisfied with how people are reacting to him. Not my parents' fault for passing on the genes and the environment that would foster suicidal thoughts sometimes.

It's my fault, is what she really thinks. My fault for not being as all-American as Ferris is, with naturally blond hair the color of spun gold, a little button nose, that small forehead, those dents in her waist that make her figure so womanly, the ability to make everything okay by smiling and bending the truth a little. My fault for not being as stubborn and manipulative, as forgiving or loving, as unabashedly like my mother as Judy is. My fault for not being a boy, like my brother. A boy who is allowed to disappoint because he isn't emotional. A boy who is allowed to have the run of the house because everyone wants him to love them. My little brother was the jewel in the family crown ever since he was born, and I believed it more than anyone. We all fought to hold him when he was a child, to pinch his cheeks, to dress him up in doll clothes and pretend he was ours. And it's my fault that no one ever wanted me to be theirs. My fault because I couldn't be as beautiful as my mother says she was before Dad ruined her with bitterness. It's my fault I have wanted to die ever since I can remember, because she never really wanted me in the first place. And she might not have wanted the others, either, but I am the ultimate failure because I cannot redeem myself to the world. There were always more reasons why I should give in than reasons I shouldn't. No one could even argue this point with me in the middle of the night when I would bring up this fact. It was true. I suppose that's the real reason I've always managed to find myself near death time and again. Because I never felt like anyone was really interested in my living anyway, least of all me. And all the pills I've taken, the psychologists, the self-help books, the meditations, Zen wishes, the jobs, the writing, the men who have nearly killed me off on their own with their lack of concern, and all the fucking lists in the world have never put me much closer to wanting to actually survive.

So just as "Here Comes the Flood" fades, I think I really will run out of these shallow breaths. That might have been okay even moments ago, but now I'm not so settled on giving in like this. The Beatles come on. "Across the Universe." And there is something soothing and grounding about the sound and the hippy-dippy words, and I start actually finding my breath again. And my heart starts to beat normally again. My ears stop ringing. I feel like I might just live. And I am smiling and taking in breaths like I've never had air in my lungs before. Like I am glad of this, for the first time I can ever remember since the thing hit me when I was a little girl. And before I turn back on to the interstate, I grab my list from the seat next to me and look at number four and smile. I cross it off and turn up the Beatles and feel better than I have since I can remember. Even if it's cheesy, even if it's just short term, four is conquered. "Decide to live."

Top Ten Things
I Want as My Epitaph

1. "I'm dead. Get off my back already." Okay, I stole that one from David.

2. "If you are reading this, you are following too closely!"

Screw this. I'm so morbid. I can't even think of anything serious. Maybe now that I think I might live a little longer, I'll have something good eventually. How about, "Keep my dentures in! I don't want to be dead without teeth!" Hopeless. Completely hopeless. I have to live longer. At least until I think of something to put on my grave.

· 19 ·

Damsel in Distress

Ah. St. Valentine's Day. I'm driving down I-40 passing an average of three armadillos per mile, heading toward Amarillo, Texas, in an old orange convertible that sounds like a sewing machine, with the top down on an overcast day to the soundtrack of, alternately, "Music Sounds Better with You" from Stardust and then "Stand Back" from Stevie Nicks. I'm feeling very pleased with myself, that I am coping so well with so much: my father's still very recent death, my lovely encounter with fire, caffeine withdrawal (well, since the last truck stop sixteen miles ago anyway), nicotine withdrawal (but every time I am tempted I think of the smell of the old lady's flesh burning and it somehow manages to kill the craving for a smoke), the first anxiety attack I've ever had, and a new fuck-it attitude about the fact that I am twenty-four years old and I have never, not even once, had a real honest-to-God valentine, least of all today. You know, the whole dinner and chocolates and tacky red lingerie and drunken sex and guilty looks from the boyfriends who do not indulge in this tradition, the bitter looks from the women who don't have a boyfriend or significant other who indulges them . . . I am sort of okay with this for some reason, all of a sudden, even if it's something I've always wanted to do. Maybe I'm just used to it by now. Maybe next year.

So I'm driving along now while "Believe" from Dig plays, and pounding on the steering wheel, driving about seventy-five, watching miles and miles of sand go by and wondering where the hell I'm going to spend the night tonight, or rather, what part of Texas, and wondering if I should splurge and actually stay someplace that has some sort of once-a-week sheet washing policy, or smoke detectors that work at the very least, when I hear a thud and my tire blows. And I am trying to gain control of the car as a huge piece of rubber flies out behind it and I'm also wondering why anything that can go wrong does with me, and thinking that maybe I was not a nun in my past life, but more likely a mass murderer who never got caught. And then I finally manage to get to the shoulder of the road and throw the damn thing in park. And I just say "fuck." It's all I can do for the next . . . oh, I don't know, five minutes. Fuck fuck fuck fuck fuckety fuck fuck fuck. FUCK!

And then I start to cry. And then I turn the stereo off finally because I'm crying and "Our Lips Are Sealed" is playing and I want to smack Belinda Carlisle and I don't want to take my car trouble out on the Go-Go's. It's not their fault my life stinks. So I turn the radio off and get out of the car to survey the damage.

As semi trucks fly past me, one nearly clipping me, I walk around to the right side and look at the front tire, or rather what was once the front tire of the Mercedes before half of it flew off about ten minutes ago. I reach up and rub the damaged tire, as if I am Starman and I can heal automobiles with my supernatural touch, and pull my hand away quickly as something moist sticks to my finger from the rubber. I put my hand to my nose, not even looking at the hand first and nearly vomit as the aroma of rotten roadkill guts fills my nostrils. I feel like a retarded version of Sherlock Holmes as I piece together that I am in fact touching roadkill guts, which, I brilliantly conclude, is the reason for my flat tire, my fucks, my queasy feeling, my newly bad attitude about St. Valentine's Day. I have hit a dead something, most likely an armadillo, judging from the recent roadside scenery. I have flattened my tire, and I now have guts on my hand, no idea how to change a tire, no fucking clue where the closest filling station is, and no desire to walk there with guts on my hand and a now throbbing migraine from lack of nicotine. I drop to the pavement and start wiping my hands against the road, rubbing them raw, and saying "Eww" like a seasoned nontraveler. I am crying over the din of the roaring trucks and facing the fact that getting a valentine is actually on my list and at this rate there is no fucking way it counts to have roadkill as a valentine and I do not want to in fact wait another year, and semis are flying by and ignoring my car and the fact that I am a damsel in distress when a hand reaches from behind me and touches my shoulder. I jump to my feet and punch a stomach and start to pull away when I look up and

recognize the face of the man who is now kneeling over, trying to catch his breath. I reach over to comfort him, to see if
I've killed him, to see if it's really who I think it is. He sits up,
now flushed and sort of looking at me like I'm a nutcase.

"Uh . . . whew." He takes a shallow breath in. "I just . . . uh . . .
wanted to know if you needed help. Aw, don't cry. Why are you
crying?"

I realize that I am still sort of sobbing a little, and at the
same time still touching this guy with, of all things, the hand
that is tainted by armadillo guts, and I pull the hand away
quickly and start to dust off his soft black T-shirt as I hear
myself say, "I just killed it."

"Killed what?"

"A dead armadillo . . . or something."

He laughs. "Oh."

"Oh, um . . . I'm an idiot. Sorry. I didn't kill it. I ran over it.
I flattened my tire." Then I add, "I haven't had a cigarette in
fourteen hours." Why do I say this?

"I just quit, too."

"It sucks."

"Yeah, it does."

I am talking to this guy about not smoking. I am stuck on
the side of the road with a complete stranger, crying, getting
armadillo guts all over him, and talking about how I don't
smoke. I need a cigarette.

"We saw you and thought you might need some help. . . . I
saw you crying . . . from the bus." He points behind him at a
huge, shiny silver tour bus with a bunch of guys peeking
through the front window, watching this exchange that has to

be a little more than comical to them. I realize again that I know this guy. I know who he is.

"I know you." He looks at me funny as I say this.

"You do?"

"Yeah."

"Are you sure? I think I would have remembered you." He's flirting. I am biting.

"Why?"

"A pretty girl like you? I would have remembered."

I blush and sort of rub my face against my shoulder. I become a cartoon character around men I am madly attracted to. "Thanks."

"So how do we know each other?"

I look at this guy standing there with wavy brown hair and his sparkly brown eyes, his cute dimpled smile, his soft black shirt, his faded black jeans, and I sort of snap out of it.

"We don't."

Now he does look confused.

"You know what? Let's get you inside the bus and we can talk about this while you get cleaned up. I know you want to wash off that hand." I nod, still sort of trying to complete a total thought without feeling like a moron and follow him to the open door of the tour bus and up the stairs. The driver is a huge white guy with a beard and a tattoo of a mermaid on his left arm. He smiles at me as he takes a sip off a diet Mountain Dew. Why do only fat men drink diet Mountain Dew anyway?

I pass a few guys who say "Hi there" and "Hey" and follow this guy to the back of the bus, past a few bunk beds and into the master bedroom of the place. He opens what looks like a tiny compartment to the right, which is actually a bathroom, and turns the faucet on for me.

"Just let me know if it turns boiling on you. This bus is sort of temperamental with visitors." He smiles and steps out of the bathroom as I slip past him and shut the bathroom door. I look at my reflection in the mirror. I'm a wreck. I've got bags under my eyes from not sleeping, I've got some sort of grease on my cheek, my eyes are fluorescent blue with red rims from crying, my hair looks as if it's in dreadlocks from having the top down. And the guts are still on my hand. I wash my hands with the almond-scented liquid soap on the sink, making sure to scrub the affected hand three times more than the other. Then I run my fingers through my hair and give up, opting for pulling it down around my face, creating kind of a semisexy "windblown" look that also makes my eyes not so noticeably red. I wipe the smudge off my cheek, take a deep breath, and whisper to my reflection, "He is a rock star. He is a mother-fucking rock star, Tyler. This is too hilarious. This is a cliché. This is a John Hughes and a Cameron Crowe movie all in one. He is totally cute and totally sweet, but he is a rock star and rock stars are assholes automatically. You have been around them your whole life and you know this, so just get a fucking grip and don't get all giggly and starstruck." I give one more nasty look and one more warning to the Tyler in the mirror. "Don't let him treat you like you're a groupie. Thank him and leave." I turn the water off.

As I open the bathroom door, he is turned toward the window, pulling his T-shirt off, revealing his soft looking, strong back, which I notice has no hair on it. I always notice the lack of flaws first, it seems. *Gee, this one has ten fingers. What luck!*

At first I kind of try to slip back into the bathroom, and then I think that maybe he wants me to see him disrobing like this on purpose, and I am thinking how unlikely it is that I will be able to be nice about telling him that I do not meet rock stars on the sides of roads in Texas, rub guts on their T-shirts and then sleep with them after I've washed up, when he turns around and pulls his shirt down quickly.

"I'm sorry. I'm just . . . changing." He seems shy. Modest.

"No, I'm sorry. For making you change." I smile and feel stupid and useless all at the same time. He walks closer to me and reaches above my head to grab a button-down corduroy shirt from a bin by the ceiling. He puts the shirt on, buttons it carelessly, and puts his arm on my shoulder.

"Don't apologize. Just don't . . . punch me again." He smiles and I melt.

"I'm sorry." I cover my mouth, as if things are just flying out of it. He laughs. I try to cover my tracks again. "I don't know why my parents didn't test me for Tourette's when I was a kid." He looks in my eyes as he laughs this time, and I feel this chemical from him that fills my entire body with electricity. He makes me smile.

"Is there a test for that sort of thing?" He's not teasing, I think he's genuinely interested.

"If there isn't, I'm sure I could write one." I throw another zinger.

"I have to know your name." He's serious.

"Why, so you can report me to the proper authorities?" I don't know why I always feel the need to perform for people.

"Well, I thought, maybe since your license plate says Tennessee, and my license plate says 'anywhere the people pay to see me' and I don't have a show tonight, if you'd like, I would like to take you to dinner. But I have to know your name so I can show you off to the rest of the guys." This all just pours forth from this guy who I just met a few minutes ago, whose shirt I have most likely defiled, who is interesting in an adorable, sweet, but very sexy and enigmatic way, and I think I am falling in love at first sight with a guy who, now that I am close enough, smells like a clean shave and touches me like I am already a dear friend. And I am not starstruck. Really. That's just stupid.

"Tyler Tracer." He shakes my hand in a mocking tone as I introduce myself.

"Well, Tyler Tracer, I'm . . ."

"I know who you are. That's what I meant when I said I knew you."

"Oh." He looks a little crestfallen, and then smiles. "Well, why don't you call me Parker? We'll pretend you don't know who I am. We'll pretend you don't know anything about me."

"Okay. . . . Why Parker?"

"It's my middle name."

"Oh. Okay." I'm not crying anymore like I was and I'm not blushing, either. He has put me at ease by trying to be anonymous, by smiling, by speaking in soothing tones. There's a knock at the door.

"Are we hitting the road soon? Jim's gotta take a dump. And I'm not putting up with another toxic waste cleanup in this bus." Parker lets go of me and opens the door.

"We have a lady in here. Shut the fuck up." Parker is half joking as he talks to the voice from the door, a long-haired, tall guy who I think plays bass in the band if I remember correctly from the video I saw a while back. The bass player looks over at me, winks at Parker, walks back along the narrow bunks to the front kitchen area and punches the guy I recognize as the lead guitarist, on the shoulder. I follow Parker out to the area where everyone is seated, except the drummer is missing, and I remember now passing by a lump on one of the bunks and figure it must be him. Parker introduces me as "Miss Tracer," as if I am a substitute teacher, and everyone sort of smiles and smirks at Parker and then me as I wave weakly. I instantly feel like Yoko Ono. I would rather feel like Jeffery Dahmer than Yoko Ono. I don't even like the band's music. It's cheesy.

"Uh, you know, Parker, I have to get going, actually."

Parker frowns. "Oh . . . do you have somewhere to be?"

I think hard on this one. I just refuse to do that groupie trip for them. Almost thirty seconds go by as everyone sort of waits for my reply. The guitar player looks like his colon might explode if I don't answer soon. He clearly needs a toilet. They did pick me up. And I don't care who he is anyway.

"No. I guess I really don't. I just don't want to leave the car . . ."

Parker waves the big tattooed driver over.

"Sharkie's got it. He'll take care of it. Where are the keys?" I hand them to Parker, who hands them to "Sharkie." He darts out of the bus like a man who once was thin and quite agile. The guys in the band get back to playing their Game Boys and carving obscene limericks into the counter. Sharkie returns with my purse, my train case, and my keys within two minutes.

"It's all locked. The top's up. There's a tire in the trunk." Parker looks over at me with a mischievous grin.

"We'll fix that when we come back." I peer over through the window at Dad's lonely car and then curiously at Parker.

"Back?"

Parker nods. "You'll see. Sharkie, take us to our final destination of the evening. I'll take care of the rest." Sharkie nods, hands me my bags, jumps back in the driver's seat, and pulls the door closed as he starts the bus again. Parker leads me back into the bedroom area and places my bags next to the bed as we pull away. I watch Dad's Mercedes get smaller through the side window as we barrel down the interstate. I plop on the bed, as if I'm already comfortable with all of this.

"I'm tired." Parker yawns while he says this, so it sounds more like "Eeeyymm teeerrrdd."

"Me, too." I turn to face Parker and rub my eyes. Another cartoon gesture. I'm getting really ridiculous.

"Well, let's sleep," Parker states innocently, as he sits on the other side of the bed. I sit up erect. He senses my discomfort.

"Tyler?"

"Yeah?"

"I'm not a jerk."

"Oh yeah? I bet you say that to all the girls you pick up on the side of the road with flat tires and guts and Tourette's."

Parker looks up at the ceiling and rubs his chin as if he's

deep in thought. "Hmm . . . no, wait . . . I don't think I've said it. . . . Wait, there was that girl in Hoboken who had a flat tire . . ." I raise my eyebrows. "But she didn't have the armadillo advantage. I kicked her to the curb."

I hit Parker on the shoulder playfully and he grabs his shoulder, as if he's fatally wounded. I look at him in all seriousness.

"If I had actually slept last night . . . or not just stopped smoking . . . or not run over roadkill . . . I wouldn't normally do this." I sound like an idiot, but I would feel like a floozy if I didn't let him know I had some reservations about taking a nap on a bed with a random rock star who picks me up on the side of the road. Parker humors me. He pulls his shoes off, lies on his pillow, and does that grin again.

"Me, neither. You can smear me with armadillo guts if I so much as think about reaching over my side of the bed . . . oops . . . already did that, didn't you?" I giggle as I take my boots off and lie down on the left side of the bed, facing Parker. He giggles, too.

I am reminded of being thirteen on my seventh grade trip to Ocoee, with the girls in tents on one side of camp, and the boys in tents on the other side of camp. And then of sneaking in one anothers' tents in the middle of the night when the counselors were in the woods getting stoned. Not for anything but innocent fun. Just for the danger of it. Just lying down and laughing. And I remember giggling like this. And all of a sudden, I feel young again. I feel young and attractive and silly . . . and sleepy. My lids slide closed with the vision of a beautiful, funny man, probably in his late twenties, with a very agreeable demeanor, in bed with me. I think of an image as I drift off, of being comforted. And for the first time in months, it's not by David.

I wake up snuggled in the crook of Parker's neck. I smell his clean scent again. I hear him swallowing. I know he's awake, but he thinks I'm still asleep. So I pretend. For him, and for me. I hear the door creak open, and Parker saying "Shh . . ." Sharkie is telling Parker they've arrived and I feel Parker's Adam's apple raise as he whispers, "You guys go on. Leave my key at the desk." Sharkie closes the door. Parker puts his hand around me protectively. I yawn, half-real, half-faking, and look up into Parker's open eyes. Parker lets go of his grip.

"You started it, you know. I tried to fight you off, but you were just having none of it." I look at Parker, puzzled, and then realize he's trying to explain why we are now in each other's arms. Suddenly, I feel uncomfortable. I sit up and smooth my hair. We're clothed. But very close.

"Where are we?" I get up from the bed and see Sharkie and a few other unfamiliars unloading suitcases from the bottom of the bus to hotel help dressed in crimson outfits outside. We are in front of a very posh hotel somewhere in Texas. Parker slides his shoes on and talks as he stretches.

"They'll check me in and everything if you want to go get something to eat now. Or a drink."

"I don't drink." It feels weird to say this. But good.

Parker mumbles, "Oh." I can't imagine he thinks we'll have any fun now. I try to change the subject.

"What time is it here?" I look out the window as if I can

somehow tell by the placement of the moon.

Parker opens the bedroom door and gestures for me to follow in front of him. "Time to go out. I want to hear about why you are in Texas. And what on earth made you buy an orange Mercedes." I giggle again as we head out of the bus and into the beautiful February night. Valentine's night and I have a date. I think I have a valentine for the first time ever. I mentally make note to mark this off my list. I think it's number nine. Right now, it feels damn near close to number one. Not quite, but almost.

Top Ten Gestures
a Guy Can Make on a First Date
That Almost Guarantee Getting Tail
by the End of the Night
(Or At Least Getting a
Really Nice Good Night Kiss)

1. Sit across a candlelit table with a twinkle in his eye, gaze longingly at the girl he's with, and say, "You are so delicate." Parker scored major points for this one. Delicate = small/thin/little/sweet/huggable/easy to pick up and carry off to bed. Call a girl delicate and she's yours, I promise.

2. Follow the lead of the girl, but take the lead when it's clear she wants him to. Parker did not order a drink because I didn't. But then he asked the waiter to concoct a very yummy nonalcoholic mixture of cranberry juice, lime juice, cherries, and soda for both of us. It was almost like a cocktail. I think I got a little tipsy psychosomatically.

3. Don't act like a superfamous rock star when the waiter and just about everyone else in the joint recognizes you as such and even says, "Aren't you . . . ?" Okay, this probably wouldn't be useful to any guys but superfamous rock stars, but I guess I mean don't be an egomaniac. Have self-confidence, but not self-inflation. It's gross. I don't care who you think you are. Basically, act like you're lucky to be with the girl you're with, but not lucky to be with just any girl at all. Parker was a pro at this. When the waiter started to ask if he was indeed

who he was, Parker said, "Yeah. And this is Tyler Tracer."
As if I was famous, too. Very smooth, I must say.

4. Ask real questions about the girl, not just "What do you
   do for a living?" or "Where are you from?" or "What
   school did you go to?" or "Do you know where the john
   is?" Parker actually asked me what my favorite thing
   about the first person I ever loved was. I thought about
   it, and realized David is the only person I thought I
   loved, and I tried to pinpoint my favorite thing about
   him. And I didn't get sad really when I considered the
   question, but I really couldn't think of an immediate
   answer. So I said the first thing that came to my mind.
   "When my father was sick and I was really upset, after he
   kind of brushed it off, he gave me the one thing I needed
   most." Parker asked what that was, and all I could say
   was "Intimacy. So much closeness that I forgot for a
   minute that someone I loved was dying. I had no idea I
   needed that direct physical relief. I thought I needed a
   hug, not wild sex." Parker said, very matter of factly,
   "Sometimes an orgasm or two is better than a hug." He
   smiled, and I smiled, because he was on the same wave-
   length. When I asked him his favorite thing about the
   first person he loved, he said, "She didn't eat paste. She
   was the only girl in first grade who couldn't stomach it.
   And so it was a lot easier to share my glue with her than
   the other girls." And he's funny, too. . . . Hmm.

5. Be witty. Don't try to be funny, but if you are, show it.
   Don't perform, just be casual. Don't tease the girl. Girls

do not, under any circumstances, like to be teased. Because if we laugh with you, we feel like doormats or bimbos. And if we take issue with your teasing, we feel like bitches. David teased me quite a bit, and this could be why he was the first guy I've ever known who made me feel like a bimbo sometimes. I am so not a bimbo.

6. Be honest, but not scathingly so. Parker and I talked about my father's death, and he was so caring and compassionate, and when I asked about his father, he said he didn't really know him all that well. Alarm signs went off in my head as I asked him why he didn't get to know him. And instead of spilling a big story about how his dad was a fucking asshole or whatever, he said, "I think it's an epidemic, really. Father and son relationships. Men have a lot of issues with each other that keep them from really being honest with each other or ever getting very close. I wish I had gotten to know him." Yes, I swear to God he said this, like he was John Gray, that relationship therapist *Mars and Venus* guy, and like he was truly healthy about the whole thing, instead of reacting like David did when I asked him about his dad, which was ignoring that the word "Dad" existed, or going off about what a horrible waste of human flesh the person was, like he did about his stepmother. I always thought the way a guy talks about and gets along with his mother is the way he views women. But I forgot that David grew up with his stepmother. So you can imagine how he most likely views women in general.

7. Have decent table manners. Parker actually placed his fork and knife in a way on the plate like Miss Manners used to say was proper to do. The exact configuration, right there on the plate, without even thinking about it. He's not formal, just polite. I was infinitely impressed. Jesus, he ate spaghetti and somehow managed to make it look graceful. This is the part where I could start thinking of our firstborn's name.

8. When the girl puts herself down, which girls are notorious for doing, do not go silent. Tell her that she isn't fat/stupid/boring/crazy and then why she isn't. Parker actually said when I mentioned my tendency to say random things and talk a lot, "I never knew that Coca-Cola used to be green. I think it's fascinating, really. Tell me something else. I'm going to start collecting these facts." Oh God, I think I can see our big house in the country now. I call Parker "Darlin'" on the phone when he calls from on tour. We have a golden retriever. I am planning our bedroom suite.

9. Offer up your dinner to taste and feed the girl little bites of it. I don't know about other girls, but there is something so sexy to me about a guy who can baby you (but refrain, for God's sake, from actual baby talk at all costs). Maybe I *am* looking for a Daddy, but whatever. Fuck off. This is my unhealthy weakness, and I don't want to get over it. Parker fed me a few bites of his rosemary mashed potatoes, and I was propelled fifty years into the future, and I got this warm feeling, thinking

LOVE IS THE DRUG

that yes, he is the sort of guy who would do this for me when I'm too old to do it for myself.

10. Act like you have no idea the girl is totally into you, even if it is obvious as she giggles at everything you say and flirts openly. David actually got to the point where he acted put out when I would compliment stupid things like how soft his hair was. Like it was too much trouble to say "thanks" or just react as if he heard me. I know I'm comparing here, but Parker, when I said his hands were beautiful, held his right palm up to my left palm, fingers against it, across the table, and said, as he looked into my eyes, "I like them because they fit with yours." I mean, this guy is like a fucking *Cosmo* profile. Except he likes me. Everything seems perfect.

Now how is he going to fuck me over?

· 20 ·

Good Night, Sweet Prince

Parker and I are sitting around the hotel pool, barefoot, swishing our feet together in the water, making ripples while the breeze blows around us. It's late, and we have now spent hours just giggling about anything and everything. Parker was a bed wetter, too. He also had a Dukes of Hazzard car. He had nightmares about the movie Angel Heart, too, and just like I did, he still watched it the next day again because the fascination with the fear was too tempting. Parker's mom was beautiful, like my mother was, and when he showed me a picture of her from the seventies, one with Parker when he was a kid, she even looked kind of similar to my mom when she was the same age. Long hair, only Parker's mom's hair was dark chestnut, a perfect smile, a well-sculpted nose like Parker's. He carries a picture of his mom and him in his wallet. But as a few alarms went off there, he told me more about their relationship and I completely related, and felt relieved. I have a picture of my mom with me, too. We both call our moms first when some-thing bad happens, just to talk. And we both get a little edgy when our mothers call just "to talk" and give us advice on, alter-nately, with Parker, a subject to write a song about, and with my mom a story I should write a book about. We talked about my art, my writing. And he was interested. He wanted to know what I wrote, when I wrote, what made me write, how many things I had written. He said he admired me because it's not glamorous like being a musician is. I told him I admired him because being a musician takes more guts. He disagreed. And I respected him because of that, too. We rambled off top ten lists for an hour. We both had the same number two for the things we will never call someone during sex ("Mama/Daddy"). The number one was too embarrassing for either one of us to actu-ally admit, but I have this feeling it was the same, too. I have talked for hours to someone about something other than David for the first time in months. And I am having fun. And I am very attracted to this person. It is a magic evening. And now I'm just swishing in the water, with my head tilted, looking up at the stars, thinking. Parker breaks the momentary silence.

"Come with me."

I look at the stars, and my eyes fill up with tears. I don't want to cry, and so of course my eyes rebel and tears start run-ning down my cheeks, and Parker reaches up and grabs the tears with his thumb, his hand resting on my chin. I apologize again. Always.

"I'm sorry. I just . . . this is all so perfect and so fucking good, and so fucked-up."

Parker nods and looks up at the stars, too, as he offers, "I know we don't know each other. But . . . well, I really want to get to know you. Really. And I'll get a separate room from yours, I'll take care of anything you need, we'll send your car back to Nashville, we'll go shopping in Paris for clothes so you don't have to send home for anything, I can show you my favorite Italian restaurant in Milan. I don't want this to end." Parker looks back over at me, and I finally make myself look him in those big brown eyes.

"Look, there's a few things, despite all of this talking, that I haven't told you." Parker waits. He's waiting for me to tell him things I don't even know the reasons for myself. I have to continue. I have to tell him why I'm in Texas finally. I don't even know.

"Parker, I'm on this . . . quest, of sorts. I told you about my dad, and although it seems like I'm running away from that, my dad left me this letter, this list, this challenge, and I have to finish it before I can go on with anything else in my life. And you are so perfect, you have no idea how perfect this all is to me, but I have these things in my life that won't go away, and some of them I don't really know if I want to push away. This man . . . he's haunting me. I loved him, Parker. I thought I loved him, anyway. I think I will always love the idea of what he could have been. And I find myself comparing you to him instead of taking you on your own merits and that's not fair to you or him, and I am so so so messed up. . . . Why the hell are you asking me to come with you? I mean, can't you tell I'm a fucking fruitcake?"

I'm sort of crying and laughing at the same time now, and Parker leans over and kisses my top lip, lightly sort of embraces my top lip with his soft full lips, and then kisses my forehead, like I've always wished on stars someone would do, like my dad used to.

He whispers in my ear, "Has anyone ever told you that you laugh like a little girl on a swing?"

I look at Parker's lips, and I want him to kiss me again, but he pulls away a little and continues. "You are a woman I would like very much to be with."

This time I lean in and start kissing him, more passionately, more familiar now, and nibble on his bottom lip, an act which before now has never been appreciated quite as much as Parker appreciates it. He exhales as if he is rising up inside himself, as if he is having a moment of tranquillity right here in front of me. He pulls away first and puts my face in his hands.

"You finish your quest. But promise me you'll tell me about it, okay? Promise me you'll tell me, when you're ready, about this list, and this man, and more about your dad."

I'm crying again, and can hardly answer. "I will. I promise."

Sharkie drives us in the bus back to my car as the sun rises white and orange over the deserts and armadillos in Texas. He changes the tire as Parker and I nuzzle, and soak in each other's essences once more. As I stand by my running car, trying to think of some reason to delay this good-bye a little longer, Parker reaches into his front pocket and pulls out one of those tiny silver folding cell phones and hands it to me.

"Take this, okay? I'm going to call you with a new number."

"Parker, I couldn't."

"Tyler, I need you to do this, please. I'll get a new phone tomorrow and call you. It will make me feel like I'm not losing you forever." Parker looks sadder than when he talked about his sister dying when he was a kid. He looks like he actually cares that I am leaving. Imagine that. I take the phone and kiss him on the cheek. He whispers almost to my eyes.

"Tyler Tracer, you are my very favorite song."

He kisses my forehead once more, opens my car door, and puts me inside. Parker walks into the bus and the doors close. As the bus pulls by, I see him looking out the side window with his hand raised, as if he's a Native American saying "How."

I reach over to the seat beside me and scratch out two things on my list. Number nine, "Get a valentine" and number three, "Do what's best for you, not what's better for the moment."

Top Ten Moments
That Make All My Past Misery
Worthwhile (Revised)

1. David and I greeting one another at Burbank Airport.

2. Hitting a dead armadillo somewhere on the I-40 in Texas.*

(*And the antics that ensued thereafter.)

· 21 ·

M.P.H.

Texas lasts and lasts and lasts. I am convinced that if Texas was a separate country, no one from the U.S. would go there very much. Not because there's really anything wrong with it. It's just too fucking big. And everyone there has their own way of doing things. I can spot a Texan a mile away no matter where I am. Their gestures are bigger, their smiles are bigger, their lives are lived on a bigger scale. I guess when you have that much space, you get accustomed to stretching everything out and it gets comfortable. Like the first time you sleep on brushed Egyptian cotton sheets with a high thread count. You never want to sleep on sandpapery cotton sheets you can get from just any housewares store again. But then you can't always afford four hundred dollar sheets, either. So you're stuck feeling like an outsider when you can't sleep at the Motel 6 anymore because you have been to the promised land of sheets and this is not it. That's how Texans must feel when they're anywhere but in Texas.

Egyptian cotton sheets aside, I got some sleep finally. Nondescript motel with plenty of smoke detectors and a nonsmoking clerk at the desk. Nonsmoking room. I've become superstitious about anything that has to do with fire now. I feel like the monster in *Frankenstein*. I slept and dreamed of sand and guts and clear aquamarine pool water and soft kisses and rough sex. All the necessary elements for my good dreams. I woke up to a beeping sound (can't I ever wake up naturally, without interruption?) and after making sure the noise was not coming from the smoke detector I had checked the batteries on three times before I went to bed, I realized that Parker's cell phone was ringing. And I didn't answer it because it could have been one of his friends or *Rolling Stone* magazine wanting to verify a quote, or his girlfriend he might never have told me about, and I did not want to explain who I was or how the hell I got Parker's phone, and while we're on the subject, why I called him Parker.

Actually, those are all excuses. I didn't answer the phone because I knew it was Parker. And I couldn't talk to him after everything that had happened. I couldn't make polite conversation and tell him that I missed him, that I changed my mind, that this whole list business was bullshit and running off to delay reality for a while in Europe until he came to his senses and shat on me in some heinous way was exactly what I wanted to do with my life right now. I couldn't tell him because one minute it was exactly how I felt, and the next minute it wasn't.

It was the next minute that scared me. Because the next minute was filled with thoughts of those cheese enchiladas and soft flannel sheets and warm, tight, but too few hugs and soft interlude kisses and the clean smell of deodorant soap

mixed with the comforting smell of sleep sweat and sex sweat and the sound of the refrigerator kicking on in the middle of the night and the feel of David's body against mine, his legs on mine, his lips on my neck, his hand resting on my tailbone, dirty words escaping my mouth into his ear and his excited reactions, the sound of the TV keeping us from revealing too much, the sound of David conquering the universe . . . that next minute was full of moments that I was willing to settle for before but no longer seemed at all acceptable. All of a sudden, they were just . . . moments. In the past. And it scared me that I forgot why I was so defeated by them and that I have replaced them with better ones so quickly. I worried that maybe Parker's moments would one day become the same. Just past mistakes. Ways to pass the time. I worried more that they weren't. That there was something more to these new moments. That I could, all over again, be giving away a piece of myself, and that this time the receiver might actually accept my offering.

I ignored the phone and became the nonconfrontational pussy I always knew I was anyway, and after it stopped ringing I tried to go back to sleep, like when I was in David's bed and the phone would ring or lightning would strike early in the morning or rain would leak through his skylight and drip drip drip until I thought I would go nuts or when that damn fly that has probably lived in his house for nine years would buzz around at 7:00 A.M. I could never do it there, either. I actually took sleeping pills every night when I stayed with him, and even sometimes also when I woke up early in the morning so I could sleep as long as David did. I wanted to live in his world, to adopt his mannerisms, to understand why his life was so

much better than mine, and why he couldn't share it with me. Why was his kind of living so valuable to him that he would give up everything else to maintain it? I still haven't figured it out. But I was always hungover in the mornings because of those damn sleeping pills. And I actually wondered why I felt so strange there, sucking down caffeine all day to wake me up. I wondered why I was always either tired or anxious, why I wanted to climb the walls or pass out for days, why I had to take two long hot baths a day. I was drugging myself to mimic David's natural state, and even still I couldn't match him. I'm too fidgety. I breathe too much.

David could seriously be in the middle of an earthquake and go back to sleep right after the big one. Actually, he's done that before. Like it never happened. He told me about it once, that the earthquake hit, knocked some shit off countertops, and rattled the house. He dozed off again as soon as the rumbling stopped. I can see him now with the covers wrapped around him. Sitting up, squinting his eyes as the boom of the ground opening up below him rumbles on, looking up through the skylight, annoyed that the earth has chosen such an inopportune moment to have a little nervous breakdown. And then fluffing his pillow, and slamming his head back down, pissed off at Mother Nature. I mean, I can have wild sex when I wake up and go right back to sleep. But otherwise, I'm up for good.

So I woke up and got my stuff together, which, to be honest, was already together and neatly waiting at the foot of my bed, just in case. I now stuff my money in the pillowcase under me, along with my keys, just in case that fabled guy with the hook I always heard about in second grade ghost stories chooses my motel room lock to pick with his mechanical limb and I need something to stab him with. No, I have not really considered the fact that a bloody, rusty hook is a lot sharper than the eroded key to the Mercedes. But it gives me a false sense of security to practice this ritual, just like I have to pull the sheets around my ears when I turn in at night, every night, so ghosts can't whisper in them (another habit from second grade). Superstition is a nice word for obsessive-compulsive disorder. I know this, and I don't care.

So now I am driving, once again. I never really get tired of driving. I pretend I'm in this big hurry to get to my destination, and then once I get there, I'm like a coke addict. Fifteen minutes later, I'm itching to do it again. So I'm trying not to rush, even though that's kind of hard when you speed like I do, but listening to Mazzy Star helps slow the pace a bit and makes me wonder, for some reason, what it must be like to do heroin. It makes me think of purple velvet poet's blouses and shooting up heroin. Nice visual. I have to pop in a new CD just to get out of my "drugs are so romantic" thinking pattern as I finally exit Texas. I am in Arizona. And I have no idea about Arizona at all, except that the sand still looks the same and I think the Arizona State University official song is "Bear Down Arizona." I used to flirt with this guy named Jade who was studying to be a lawyer and worked at juvie in Nashville in the meantime, and I called him Bear Down Jadey because we were drunk one night and he sang me his school song and I thought the title was so funny. I thought about two things as I drove the first few miles through Arizona: That *Bear Down Jadey* could have been a great

name for a gay male porn flick and that's why Jade must not
have thought it was as hilarious as I did when I started singing
it, and that my nickname for years after that night was Hot
From Liquor, which totally explains so many stupid antics of
the pre-reformed, self-diagnosed, alcoholic, young, dumb, and
full of come Tyler Tracer after that date. God, is it possible that
I really can tell a difference between age twenty-three and
twenty-four? I feel so much older. Almost wiser. But then, time
is no match for misery. Misery is the cause of wrinkles and
death of most people in the end. And maturity. I'd rather be
immature and happy any day.

"Brass in Pocket" is now playing, the Suede version that
should have been the original version it's so fucking good. The
Pretenders ought to just give that one to them. And I drive.
And drive some more. And as I'm speeding past what look like
adobes or whatever those mud houses are called, I spot a lump
on the side of the road coming up, and I slow down to see what
it is because it's moving, unlike the lumps that don't move and
always end up being dead armadillos. And I see that it, too, is
an armadillo, but it's not dead. Injured, but not dead. And I
have to stop.

As I tiptoe to the other side of the car, I have my keys in
hand as if I can use the same superstition policy I have for
invisible hook men on a rabid armadillo. But as I get to the
shoulder and get closer, I see that the poor thing isn't rabid,
he's hurt. His foot is kind of bleeding, and he's biting at it, and
I instantly get all sad and am reminded that "the natural order
of things" is the worst excuse for the suffering that animals go

through for our convenience. The conventional idea that nature should be allowed to run its course, especially when humans are around to fuck it up, is bullshit, just like the idea that men aren't supposed to cry (even though I hate seeing men cry) and the notion that spanking teaches children anything except how to physically take out their own inadequacies on other people in later life. And I have to do something. I just have to. So I run over to the trunk and get David's old plaid button-down shirt he gave me and scoop the armadillo up in it, cradling his midsection while trying not to get my hands near his mouth, just in case. He sort of squeals, and I know that I've got to help him out. I've officially made the thing a "he" already. The codependent girlfriend comes out in me every time.

I lay the little guy on the seat next to me and realize that he's been hit by someone who most likely did not see him running out there, probably because they were barreling down the highway going nearly as fast as I do, and I know that it might kill me to slow down (or more likely save me from getting killed), but it is on my list, after all, so I have to do it sometime, and it's such a trivial thing compared to so many other bigger issues I have. I make a promise to this injured armadillo lying on the passenger seat, bleeding all over David's shirt, as I mentally mark off number eight.

"I promise I won't speed anymore."

The armadillo won't hold me to it, but Dad will. I take my foot off the accelerator and start living life in the foreign world called "The Speed Limit Zone." God, I already hate this.

Top Ten Best Things
About Driving Fast

1. You get wherever you're going faster.

2. It feels rebellious to speed.

3. 55, 65, 70 miles per hour? Please. It's just too slow on an interstate that has no curves or bumps for two hundred miles and there's nothing to do but stare at sand passing by, maybe a lone gas station with a wooden Indian and fake moccasins every fifteen miles. Speeding while driving is like getting hammered before you play Monopoly. It adds a new challenge to the mix, makes life a little more interesting.

4. It makes me feel in control of something because, honestly, I'm not in control of anything at this point, it seems.

5. Convertible top down + stars + desert air + high speeds + good tunes = a moment of peace. A piece of goodness.

6. You can't listen to Soundgarden and go thirty-five in a residential area. It's bullshit. It makes you feel like a sellout.

7. Aggression. It's like when I run. I don't walk, I don't jog, I bust out running and test my body until my legs feel like they will indeed fall off, and I'm panting, and pushing my body way past the point of "no pain, no gain," and I know that's why I've had shinsplints and blisters and sprained ankles and sore muscles for days, but I have to run. I have to take advantage of what I have

because one day, I won't have it anymore. And I have to get out my anger somehow.

8. Sometimes, I honestly don't even mean to speed. I don't even notice it at all. I know, it sounds like a terrible excuse—"Officer, I just didn't see the speedometer"—but really, it just feels natural to go as fast as you can.

9. What's that 140 on the speedometer for if not for using?

10. Self-destruction. It all goes back to this. Everything I do is really, in essence, to destroy myself. Not as much for the romance, like James Dean did in Chalome, driving Little Bastard far too fast for those hills in California because he was supposed to, because he knew better than anyone else that he was fairly miserable, that he was an artist, and just like David bought into that crap, that he was somehow supposed to die too soon. Not for the legend of it, but because everything I do is a way to hurt myself, because not only am I a masochist, I am a masochist with a lead foot.

· 22 ·

The Transfusion

Petey is bloody. I am bloody. The front seat of my car is bloody. David's shirt is bloody. I'm actually glad David's shirt is bloody. It looks like it should. War wounds from feelings he refused to acknowledge. The blood of things unsaid. The blood I tried to hide in the wash the first time menses attacked. The blood my father sucked out of me with his vampiric lifestyle. The blood I've offered up to any takers. The blood of innocence, of something covered in scaly spines to protect itself from spiky intent. Petey is dying. I have been, too, only the blood hasn't been pouring out of me until now. It's been poisoning me from the inside out for as long as I can remember. I have to get rid of this blood.

Have you ever cut your finger and sucked on it to stop the bleeding? It makes no sense, but you do it because it seems natural. To consume yourself with yourself. Like a bitch licks the afterbirth off her puppy. But do you eat your own shit? No way. Snot? Gross. Spit? Eww. Sweat? Jesus, we spend billions a year to avoid that fluid from getting out. Now menstrual blood, yes, we find appalling as a general rule, but only because it is only a woman's kind of expelling and men do not like to acknowledge, accept, or—God forbid—approve of something that only women have. But human blood is sacred. Just look at how we're forced to accept people we are connected to by blood that normally we would have restraining orders against.

I never take an injury seriously unless I see blood. Hence, the reason I let so many things go in the past. When Dad yelled at my mother, called her a whore, told her how stupid she was, how worthless she was, how trapped he was in "us," he never drew blood. So I never knew those wounds needed attending. When he was dying, I saw no blood. I never really believed he was sick, I guess. Well, maybe sick, but not *dying*. Dying was all about people in car crashes with organs ten feet from their bodies and bloody windshields. I guess I have been acting all along as if Dad's not really dead, he's just not speaking to me anymore.

I want, for once in my trivial fucking existence, to do something to get back at this thing that rules me, this sickness of moods. It has dragged me down for long enough. I have become apathetic, bitter, battered, used goods. The rest becomes an act. For small moments, I am content. For tiny particles of time I think it's all okay. I get a kiss, a compliment, a job, a triumph thrown at me. But it's just not enough.

I called home when I stopped to get Petey some water. Mom was full of questions. I wanted to know one thing. I wanted to

know why Dad left so soon when he seemed to be doing a little better. The autopsy results had come back. I should have
never asked. He would have been okay if he hadn't given in to
the dance. He would have lived if he hadn't still been using. It
kills me that this man who had a chance to fix everything
decides to throw it all away for a fucking high. He takes it all,
throws it up in the air, looks at us with a smirk, and says, "Fuck
it." I would have been angry before. But I understand now. I get
it. Drugs and booze were Dad's "thing." They kept him from
facing his own battles with the depression beast. They were the
thing to keep him away from the real "thing." And he just
couldn't live with any of it anymore. The desire to escape was
too attractive. He was tired of it. So am I.

My blood has been poisoned by my father's genes, my family's burdens, my own shortcomings. I want to rid myself of
this poison, even if it means I don't survive the removal. I
picked up the first sharp object I found on the shoulder. A broken Pabst Blue Ribbon beer bottle. How fitting is that? They
don't even have PBR in Arizona. This came from someone
from my neck of the woods. They left it for me here. Dad
would be proud. Self-destructive *and* appropriate. I sat in the
front seat for a while, skimming the edge along my fingers,
making tiny cuts that stung, preparing myself for the big cut. I
carried Petey out to the side of the car, in the gravel. There's no
preparation for the ceremony of destroying oneself. No pro-
crastinating. You just have to dive right in. I pressed the brown
edge against my wrist until I saw puckers of skin on each side
and I dragged the glass along like this thing has dragged me
along. Slowly. Purposefully. The blood first came in beads. I

dragged again and then dropped the glass in pain. The blood began to flow. And now it's running out of me.

Finally, with the blood that is leaking out from my arm, so does the poison I've been holding all this time: Dad comes home in the middle of the night, drunk again. Mom tells us he's drunk, that he's screwing that bitch he met at the studio, that she is going to leave. I am three years old. I don't know what screwing means. It sounds like something bad, though. She doesn't leave. He tries to come in the house. She threatens him with the Red Rider BB gun. He retreats. She makes him sleep out in the van. I go to visit him at two in the morning. Mom wants me to see if he's still alive. I climb in through the window. He's alive. He's slurring his words. He's not sure if it's me or my sister he's talking to. I am afraid of my father. I am afraid he is going to hurt me. I am afraid the monster that makes him drink, makes him throw things at Mommy, makes him say mean things, and hide fifths of vodka in his boot, that the same monster that does these things is going to come at me. Do something bad to me. He smells funny. He looks at me funny. I try to climb out the window. He grabs my foot. I escape. He gets my slipper in his hand. I remember this slipper as I bleed. What happened to this slipper?

Other images. Being little, hoping Mommy won't kill herself. Hiding all the knives under my bed and staying up all night watching over her. Waiting until the sun comes up. If the sun comes up, I'm safe. She will live. She will decide to live for me. She will live for the glow of the sunlight on my face. I can't remember why Mommy wanted to kill herself that time. There were so many times. I think of someone watching over me all night, making sure I don't do myself in. No one has. There are so many times. And no one will.

I think of pretending. I think of all the years I played house, I pretended I was famous. I pretended I was older. I pretended I had breasts. I pretended I was married. I pretended to smoke. I pretended the baby dolls were children. I pretended that one day I wouldn't have to pretend. I'm still pretending. I've been pretending the whole time. Pretending I would die if someone didn't love me. Pretending that sex meant he loved me. Pretended that if I wrote the words, they would come true. Pretended that it was all okay. Dad's disease was okay. I pretended it was like when he made himself sick from drinking. I pretended it would go away after he vomited. He would vomit his liver and grow a new one. I pretended when he was sick that the delusions of grandeur he had were normal. But I couldn't pretend he wasn't gone. I pretended I liked it when boys wanted to see under my skirt. I pretended I was full of surprises. I pretended I wanted to live for so long. I pretended the word "bubbly." I pretended I loved things I didn't understand. I pretended I was not shocked when that boy shoved himself inside me even though I said no. I pretended I wanted it. I pretended it was my fault. I pretended to come. I pretended to come so many times. I thought I would never really come. I pretended to take comfort in things about my life that were not okay. I pretended I didn't want to be domestic. I pretended I liked to be alone. I pretended I was independent. I pretended I didn't like it when David was weak, when he needed me. I pretended he wasn't eating me up when he was short with me. I pretended I thought he was perfect. I pretended not to notice the condom wrapper I found under his bed when I was cleaning. I pretended I wasn't obsessing over when he used the condom, where he used it, who he used it on. Was she prettier? Did she smell better? Did she scream louder? How long did he fuck her? Did she have dark sun-kissed breasts and long black hair? Was that the hair I picked up off the carpet? I pretended I wasn't jealous of every single person who now got to come in contact with David because I couldn't. I pretended I was going on. I pretended I wasn't falling for Parker. I pretended I wasn't comparing him to David. I pretended that I could openly trust a good situation. I pretended I didn't hear the cell phone ring again in the car. I pretended I didn't know why I was really on this road trip. I pretended I didn't want to drink anymore. I pretended all that mattered in life was love. I pretended David was telling the truth. I pretended I believed someone could save me from me. I pretended the whole mess of mistakes I have made are simply experience. I pretended to like experience. I exhale my pretense, my pretending. I bleed it out.

David rubbing my hair, Parker stroking my feet, Dad putting both arms around me when he hugged me when I was fourteen and told me I was chubby, me still needing that hug, even though it was attached to a sword that dug deeper than anything else had done. The feel of David inside me, the feel of his lips when he kissed my neck, my back. Part adoration, part obligation. The feel of my cat's fur the first time I did X on that snowy night. The feel of baby's skin. The smell of smoked oysters and drunkenness. The color of the blood they drew out of me at the hospital when I was sick for that year. My blood was purple. I thought if I could change it to a bright red color, the suggestive thoughts that told me to die would go away. The feeling of being a miserable teenager, being self-conscious, of thinking people were looking at me like I was an ugly rock in an otherwise pretty garden. The feeling of being sexy, of wearing soft, fitted things against my bare skin, of being touched with interest instead of pity. The feeling that naked was good. Naked skin against naked skin was safe. The smell of his wanting. The sound of mine. The words I said and was sorry. The words I never could say at the right time. The pieces of my heart I wanted back. The music I invested my memories in. The love I gave and gave and gave and gave.

Everything that was taken from me is gone. But so are all these things. They are now outside of me, in a puddle around me. I am in the same place I was so long ago, just like I thought in that water, drowning when I was younger at the Narrows of the Harpeth. I think of the only important thing that weighs me down. "I wonder . . . I wonder if I'll live." The last image I remember is of Petey licking blood off of me, like a thirsty dog. And of red. Of puddles and puddles of poisonous red.

When I come to, the sun is blinding me. I am still lying face-up in gravel, but I am alive. I actually feel more alive than I ever have. My wrist is cut, but the blood is dried to me. Black almost.

Petey is . . . not so alive, motionless a few feet from me. When I get up and move to where he is lying, I see the puddle I imagined myself lying in earlier, around him, coming from his mouth. Far more blood than an armadillo could ever hold. I see pictures in my head of some wounded armadillo drinking my poison and giving me his healthy fluid in return. Like some totally sick bestiality vampire flick or something. I am crazier than I thought. But I am alive. And Petey is the reason. I have been saved and I saw no bright lights, no figures walking through a tunnel. Just a few cheesy eighties characters and an armadillo licking my arm. I scoop Petey's lifeless body in David's soaked shirt, and get back in the car. This was on my list, as much as I never wanted it to be. To receive real love, to have it reciprocated, to heal. My true love was a mammal closely related to an anteater. And he was the most beautiful creature I have ever met.

Top Ten Religious Experiences

1. The first sex with David. I'm sorry. It was just a moment for me. Still is. Sex with love. Quite religious for me.

2. Waking up the first morning I hadn't wet the bed. I was a teenager. It had haunted me since birth. It was like being crippled and one day waking up and walking out of bed. I think I must have been sixteen almost.

3. The first time I took Ecstasy. I'm not going to pretend it wasn't the best drug I've ever done in my life. But then, I could never feel the way I felt the first time. After that it was just something to do.

4. The first time I wrote something, and when I came back and read it the next day, had no idea where it came from. The first time the muse entered and took over for me.

5. The first time I heard Jeff Buckley.

6. That one Christmas I sang in choir and performed at St. Henry's for midnight mass. I'm not religious, and certainly not Catholic, but that was beauty. Utterly ridiculous, over-the-top, coveting beauty. I loved it.

7. The first time I felt buzzed but not drunk. It was fuzzy. It was happy. Nothing mattered but the feeling.

8. My first orgasm, after watching *9½ Weeks*, having a beer, smoking a cigarette, and finally, much later than anyone I knew, thinking about myself, about pleasing myself. The glow that lasted for three days afterward. People actually said I looked different.

9. Forgiving my father and realizing we had a relationship finally after nineteen strained years. That first time I said "I love you" to him and thought that I meant it.

10. Exchanging blood with an armadillo. Petey's sacrifice.

· 23 ·

Number One

The Valley is like a hyper reality. Like the Internet. One hour equals one normal human East Coast day. No one feels like they're aging here until it's too late. Every time I've been to L.A. and back, I have worse jetlag than anyplace else. It takes me weeks to switch back to being a normal person again. All the way through Arizona, all the way to California, to the Valley, I think about this. That I have driven to another planet. NASA is a waste of time. Just give someone a few hundred bucks to study L.A.liens. They're a breed unto themselves. No one is born in L.A. If you are, your daddy is famous, or your mommy is rich and divorced. If neither one of these apply, you need to move or become a struggling rock star/actor/performance artist/poet. These are the rules. I don't make them up. I think they were etched on the Hollywood sign a long time ago.

And in the Valley, you have to assume your role, too. You must feel better than people who live directly in L.A., because you are just outside it. You must talk about them as if you are not one of them. You must say you hate L.A., even though you never really plan on moving. You must pretend that looks don't matter, though you live in L.A. simply because it's beautiful. You must learn plastic. Plastic hellos, plastic how are you's, plastic tits, plastic hair, plastic relationships, plastic I love you's. This all being said, I love L.A. I love the Valley. They're so behind, so hedonistic, so Roman, it's chic. It's a great place. I realize that I'm glad I made the trip when I pass by a woman in her twenties in Gucci holding a baby in what could only be Gucci and walking next to her husband who must be seventy, on his cell phone, who is staring at the even younger, complete stranger chick with a nice ass who walks by. He can't appreciate his current good fortune. There is too much other good fortune around here to be had. This is the mantra in the Valley.

I am driving the streets and I don't need to look at the map anymore. I know this place. I walked for hours and miles and days around here. I could walk around here in the dark and still find my way. I know the way each street smells, the plants in the yards. I drive and breathe. I try to remember why I'm here. Try to not have another anxiety attack. Try to be brave. I've never been brave. Just bold. Boldness has gotten me anyplace I've ever been. Bold sent me here. Bold is going to get me where I'm going. Hopefully, bold will get me out of the car when I get there.

Petey is in Arizona being "prepared" by a company I found in the Arizona Yellow Pages that advertised FREEZE-DRY TAXI-

DERMY! READY IN AS LITTLE AS 45 DAYS! He had become the best road companion I ever had. Supportive, reverent, quiet. Very quiet. I bet he'll be kind of shiny when he's ready. Shellacked or something. The guy asked for a description and a photo of him "before." I didn't know what to tell him. I just want to have him with me. I don't care if it's creepy. So is what happened.

I am in David's neighborhood. I pull down the dead end street. Pass that black SUV in the yard next door. Pass the FOR SALE signs and a girl posing for photos in her own yard in spandex. I pull over and park. I look in the mirror, and don't even care. I'm here. I'm chasing my number one. I am making my fate, getting the final answer, hoping for a love story no one could predict. Hoping that I don't pass out before I get to the door.

I am walking. I am counting my steps like I used to do before I opened that little white gate, slowing down, trying to stay away longer. I am repeating in my head, "Number one, number one, number one." I am at the gate. David's car is parked out front. He's here. I know he's here. I pull the latch open and tiptoe past the duplex's plastic table and chairs, past the neighbor's old motorcycle. I count the bricks on the way to his little green door. I can hear the TV. I can hear a video game. The curtain is cracked. I peek in.

The shelves are still on the right side, on the wall. The couch is still parked in front of the closet. The TV is still in that little space across from the bed. I see David's legs dangling over the edge of the couch. I see smoke rising above him. He's listening to the television while he plays a game. His dinner is probably in the oven while he plays. I can smell

Italian and dirty clothes. He probably doesn't notice it's evening. He probably doesn't notice he's been playing the game for the last six hours. He probably doesn't realize he's been doing the same thing for the last six years. He probably has no idea that I am seeing all this again, that it all looks the same. That even if I was inside instead of outside, for all intents and purposes, it would be the same. Only I would be in the way. I would be holding up this routine. I would be breathing. I would be taking away the air he didn't want to share. I see David turn around and look at the TV. He's wearing those glasses and that velour shirt. He's cold. He hasn't cut his hair. He hasn't washed it. He is moping. He's been moping since he moved to L.A. It was not what he expected it to be. I was not what he expected me to be. He wasn't what I expected him to be. I was willing to change what I expected. He wasn't. He's not mine. He never was mine.

I came here, I drove across the country to be with him. I thought I loved him. I thought I loved him more than I love anyone I've ever known. I wanted to save him. I wanted to rush in, pick him up, and carry him off to the mountains, feed him wildflowers and Keats until all that anger, all that sadness, all this routine of dying went away. He is planning his death here. He is pretending every day is the same so he doesn't have to age and face the end. And I came here to save him. I came here to ask him to save me. Save me from my dependence on him, convince me he wasn't as great as I made him out to be. At the very least, I came here to burst in, beg him to talk to me, and hear the final word, "no." I came here for an answer to why he couldn't see I was kinging him. He had free reign over the board now. He could go wherever he pleased. Jump all over me a million times. Do double jumps. I came to see why anyone who was winning the game just got up and left before it was over. Before getting the prize. I came to make him happy because I thought that's what would make me happy. I look at him eyeing the TV suspiciously. Lighting another cigarette. Pissed off that the world does not operate like he does. I look at his face once more. I memorize the expression. It's the same one he gave me when I left the last time. "Go away." And I said out loud what I have been thinking for a long time now.

This can't make me happy.

Before David sees me, I pull my face from the window. I take David's bloody shirt from my grip, the shirt he gave me that time I was folding his laundry and I admired it. Thinking of what David must have looked like when he wore this plaid shirt. The one he said was a nice one. The one he said I could have. The one that Petey gave his life away on. The part of David, the part of me, the part of my pain, the part of my healing that is now over. I tie it around his doorknob and walk away.

I want David to heal. I want the world to see him as I did, the saint of art, the angel in black, the sweet boy who smiled and told me forever wasn't long enough for us. The lover. The icon. The friend. I wanted so much to be with him, to help him fight his battles, that I forgot I have my own battles. I pretended I was pursuing my number one, when really I was pursuing his.

To get him out of this. To heal him. But I can't heal him. That's not on my list anymore. Maybe he'll go on his own journey. Maybe one day he can bleed his anger, his unfairness, his sadness out. But I have to be happy. And this is not the answer to that last item I was chasing. Not making someone else force themselves into chasing happy. I have to find my own. I give him his shirt, now touched with healing, and hope for the best. I hope happiness for him. I touch his door one last time and know that I will remember David for the rest of my life.

I tiptoe back to my car, crying a little. I will always think of David and cry a little. He is like the saddest movie you've ever seen because you're the audience and you can see the problems that are coming up ahead for him. But he's the character in the movie. He won't listen when you yell, "Go to the door! Tell her you'll love her to death!" He can't hear you. He's stuck in the movie.

I climb in and turn off the radio. I don't need music. I have my own sound track going on in my head. I want to remember what L.A. sounds like to someone who is finally letting feigned love go. I drive up Mulholland and back on to the freeway. I look over at my list. That fucking number one. "Do what makes you happy." It is all I've ever wanted.

I figure I can wait a while. I have the rest of my life to finish number one, I suppose. Dad, I've grown. Just on this trip I've grown. I want more and I want less out of life. I won't settle for finishing someone else's list for them, like I tried to do with so many men, so many friends, and you. I wanted to help them with their lists because I wanted them to help me with mine. I wanted us to have lists together. But they were all selfish. And so were you. I'm making new lists. Lists of things I've done that I love to do that are good for my body, better for my soul, reasons I'm going to love being who I am when I'm old. Reasons to wake up tomorrow morning and say, "Goddamn, I'm so happy I could scream!" I'm going to list reasons why I must have loved you so much. I'm going to list reasons I'm going to tell my children, "You should have met your grandpa. He was a good man. He was my daddy. You have his shoulders." I'm going to live for moments, instead of memories. I'm going to concentrate on the journey now, instead of the mission.

Epilogue

Beep! Beep! Beep!

"Hello?"

"Parker?"

"Oh God . . . Tyler? You got my message."

"Wow, you knew it was me."

"I don't have a garbage can full of cell phones I give out to girls who slime me with guts, you know. I had it narrowed down to you or—"

"That girl from Hoboken?"

"Ten points for remembering bad jokes!"

"So how many points do I have now, Parker?"

"You have no idea. Somewhere in the millions."

"Really . . ."

"How's the mission?"

"Mmmm . . . you wouldn't believe me if I told you."

"I've got all the time in the world. I'm quite gullible, too.

Lay it on me. Tell me about the list. Did you get all the items checked off?"

"Oh . . . well, yeah, actually. Except this one thing . . ."

"What is it? Maybe I can find it here in London."

"Oh God, Parker, it's not something you can buy! It's just . . . it's going to take a long time to get this one. But I think I'll like trying to find it as well as just happening upon it. I think I'm on my way already."

"Where are you on your way to right now? I mean, literally."

"Oh . . . I hadn't really thought about it. I'm on the L.A. freeway. Passing the Staples Center downtown."

"Got it. Hold on a sec . . . Sharkie!"

"Parker? Hello?"

"Okay. Do you know where LAX is from there?"

"Yeah. I do. Why?"

"Hey, Tyler, do you think you could do a little looking here . . . around Europe?"

"What are you saying?"

"I'm saying there's a ticket at LAX waiting for you, if you want it. Maybe I can help you finish this list off. Maybe you just need some support."

"That's all I've ever wanted, really. Support."

"Hey, Tyler?"

"Yeah?"

"How are you really? Are you okay?"

Maybe this happy thing won't be so hard after all.

Top Ten Things
I Want to Do in Life

1. ~~Do what makes you happy.~~ Get support. And good backrubs.

2. Have true love reciprocated.

3. Do what's best for you, not what's better for the moment.

4. Decide to live.

5. Heal.

6. Stop smoking.

7. Get out of Nashville.

8. Stop speeding.

9. Get a valentine.

10. Stop drinking.